Rajan Kumar Patel was born into exile du 1972. His parents first took him to India f where he was raised.

A graduate of London's Bartlett School of Architecture and Planning, Rajan is a qualified Urban Town Planner.

In between writing *FEAST OF VARANASI* and his epic trilogy series *THE RISHI SCROLLS,* he has written the screenplay for, then produced and directed his debut British feature film, *FEAST OF VARANASI* released in 2016.

He lives with his wife Ketal and two sons, Aryan and Aarush, in London.

This book is dedicated to Banaras.
A place that has existed long before me and will remain long after I have passed.
My words are fleeting thoughts in its eternal presence.

Cover design by Roberto Vivancos

First published in Great Britain in 2016 by Dreamit Filmit Ltd.

Discover more about the feature film by visiting - **feastofvaranasi.com**

To find out more about *The Rishi Scrolls* book series, visit - **therishiscrolls.com**

CONTENTS

Feast of Varanasi

TO HAVE NOTHING, IS EVERYTHING

By

RAJAN KUMAR PATEL

Mark Twain wrote of his time in Banaras:

'It is older than history, older than tradition, older even than legend, and looks twice as old as all of them put together.'

'For me, Banaras is Banaras: timeless.'

Rajan Kumar Patel

To live and die in the city of pyres,

you by my side under its flaming sky,

we rise together into the heavens

forever free until the starlight dies.

ONE

Midnight, District of Varanasi, India

The first sound she heard was crickets, chirping under the cover of a half moon. Her blurred vision slowly pieced together the foggy image of the man who had taken her. As her eyes opened, she remembered what had happened. Fear gripped her broken body.

She was unable to move. Her hands and feet were bound, and she was gagged by a tight cloth reeking of petrol fumes. In the grim darkness, barely lit by a single candle, the face of her abductor appeared through the fading swirls of cigarette smoke.

The girl's name was Devika. Three days earlier she'd celebrated her twenty-second birthday with friends. Now she found herself at the mercy of a demon. Unable to meet his eyes, she pushed back on her bare heels, scraping the floor until she hit a wall. Her eyes darted from side to side, looking for a way out, but none existed.

Devika's breathing steadied as she realised her life depended on his will. He was twitchy. He fiddled with an emerald ring on his finger. He had the strength to take her but a lingering compassion had, until now, held him at bay. He did not consider his actions evil, but a necessary sacrifice to complete his journey. He stubbed out what remained of his cigarette and looked at his wristwatch, watching the hand as it ticked, second by second, around the face until the midnight hour turned Saturday to Sunday – the day of sacrifice.

It was time.

He started by emptying the contents of his sports bag. One by one he carefully arranged the items on the dull metal skin of an oil canteen. By the guttering candle, he placed a bushel of fresh jasmine flowers, incense sticks, a small tin of deep red powder, a small photograph of a smiling girl, a copper pot filled with holy water, and a threaded chain of Tulsi (basil) leaves. The fresh scent of jasmine and Tulsi leached across the room to Devika. Her eyes pleaded with him. Ignoring her, he set about the task he had planned – and perfected. She was not the first, nor would she be his last.

After lighting the incense stick, he began with the photograph. He seemed lost in its lure, his thoughts shifted to happier times. A brief smile came to his face; a tear swelled in his eye as he touched the face on the photograph. He then dipped his thumb in holy water and took the red powder and rubbed it between his fingers. Then he brushed a stroke of bright red across the girl's forehead. When he was done, he placed the marked photograph down with care. Next he took the Tulsi and inhaled its scent close to his face, calming any doubts. Then he turned to Devika, who was unable to kick him away. He placed the Tulsi around her neck and held her firm, eye to eye. Her muffled cries beneath the cloth left him unmoved.

He took the petrol drum by his side and emptied it over Devika. The rope tore her skin as she tried to break free. The room filled with the sound of petrol splashing on the floor, and her choking rage. It ended abruptly with the striking of a single match. In that moment between life and death, Devika saw nothing else but the flame as darkness crowded in on her from all sides. She heard the sound of crickets once more as the flame danced across the room and struck her, giving birth to a fireball – and, with it, the sacrifice.

He gave the gods a feast of fire. He watched as the fire engulfed the corner of the room. The life beneath the flames was gone. And when all was done, he curled back into the darkness and whispered under his breath, 'You're free now.'

TWO

Evening, London

'You're free now.' Helen mouthed in silence. Her mother Sarah's last words, scribbled on a notepad moments before she drowned her pain with an overdose of whisky and pills, leaving behind her only daughter, Helen, and her husband of twenty-five years, Jack.

Helen worked as a teacher in a local school. She was still on probation, having only taken up the post three months earlier. Until a fortnight ago she'd been living with her mother but she'd moved out after an argument. Her father was rarely home. In recent years he'd become distant, flaunting other women, each fling more open than the last. He had a particular fondness for younger girls. His last had been barely eighteen. Sarah put up with it as she'd always done, for the family. Jack always managed to crawl his way back; it made her feel needed until the next girl came along. After Sarah's death, he'd vanished. His absence didn't bother Helen; in fact, she was relieved. She had no affection towards him, no fond memories, no bond. He had missed his wife's funeral. Only Helen and Cathy, her mother's best friend, were present. In a church built for one hundred, the priest's voice had echoed in the void.

Outside Sarah's home, the restless rain finally stopped. The greyish clouds hanging low over the rooftops of suburban London briefly cracked and, through the gaps, rays of sunlight pierced. A flash of light hit the first-floor window of the house, and the glare turned Helen's eye away from her mother's letter, still clutched in her hand, towards an oil painting hanging over the dressing table. It was a delicate piece, no bigger than a book. In its oily sheen her face appeared. Gazing at the picture, Helen found herself remembering Sarah's last words to her. Words spoken by a wounded soul after a dagger was plunged into her heart – a dagger thrown by her daughter. But there had been no blade. Just words, each one cutting and painful: words no mother should have to hear from her daughter.

And now Sarah was dead. Helen felt responsible.

Having said nothing for years, she desperately tried to find the trigger to let it all out. But she couldn't, and now she felt guilty of causing Sarah's death. She wished that things could go back to the way they were, but it was too late. In the darkness, Sarah found a way out – and she left Helen a path to hers.

The oil painting was of a faraway place in North-East India: Varanasi's burning *ghats*, a stretch of holy steps connecting the land of the mortals with the immortal River Ganges. It showed dark, bony, gaunt men working amid raging funeral pyres that were lined up along the banks of the Ganges. One was smashing a roasting skull with a charred stick, while another stoked the fires. It was as old as she was, sent by her aunt to her mother soon after her aunt had arrived in Varanasi. Helen had never met her.

A voice from behind Helen broke the silence.

'I've brought you some tea,' said Cathy, placing the teacup and biscuits on the table. She could see Helen was lost in the painting.

'You're going to have to tell her.'

'I know,' replied Helen.

'I still remember her. She was beautiful, just like your mother. I never understood why she left.'

The phone rang in the room next door.

'I'll get it,' said Cathy. As she left the room Helen unhooked the painting from the wall and placed it in a cardboard box along with other memories of her mother, including her last letter, and favourite pendant. She then walked down the stairs.

'It was no one, dear. Just a cold caller. I told them not to call again, but they rarely listen,' said Cathy, coming back to an empty bedroom to find the tea and biscuits untouched. Shortly afterwards, she heard the front door close. Helen was gone.

She made her way back to her place. It was a pokey loft room in an old Victorian pub: with rents so high, it was all she could afford. As it began to drizzle once again, the light faded inside. Raindrops tapped against the roof light; the kettle stewed on the side table. Warmed by a mug of fresh tea, she pulled out the painting. She had little wall space, but she found a spot between her bed and desk and hung it up. Slumping back in her chair, Sarah's letter came to her mind.

> *You're free now. I want you to live the life you deserve – free from the past, free from him. I want you to find Aunt Agatha and take this pendant to her. She'll know why I sent you. Trust me, Agatha is your future now. Do this for me, Helen, for your mother.*
>
> *Mum*

Helen went back to the box and found the pendant: a dull, pear-shaped emerald threaded through with leafy silver stems. She hadn't seen it for many years. It was in need of a thorough polish to bring back its shine. Helen hung it around her neck. Lying back in her chair, she stared up at the roof light. The grim grey view looked sterile; a far cry from the saffron fires of the oil painting.

THREE

Shielded from the choking fumes of Delhi's traffic, a quiet forensic analyst was busy at work. His small office was tinged in amber from the passing light filtering through the blinds he'd fitted himself to hide the polished sheen of the cobalt windows. The furniture was basic, a touch rustic for a newly built government building glazed from floor to floor. The analyst, absorbed in observing a postage stamp, failed to notice the tea boy come in with a roasting cup of morning chai – at least, that's what the tea boy thought as he made his way out the door.

'Wait,' said the analyst.

The tea boy stopped.

'Come back.'

The tea boy did as he was asked and stood in front of the analyst, who was still observing the stamp, which he held firmly with tweezers in one hand. He wore a white glove and in his other hand held a magnifying glass. His right eye, magnified through the glass, glanced up to the tea boy.

'Tell Raman' – the chai stall owner, who operated just outside the building – 'If the price of tea bags has gone up, then up his price, but don't send me chai made from out-of-date tea bags.'

He had a strong sense of smell, and the tea lacked any odour.

'Sorry, sir. It won't happen again. I'll get another one.'

'Leave it – I'll let it go this time.'

'No sir, I'll get you another one – best one, sir.' The tea boy left. After all, *he* hadn't made it; it gave him an excuse to scold his boss, who was unlikely to make the same mistake again. The analyst was no fan of the assortment of tea bags, from Darjeeling to Early Grey, lined up neatly inside the canteen's tea box. He preferred the sugar-laced chai, punchy and dark, hand-delivered piping hot, in a shot glass, brewed by the street merchants down below. It made him feel he was still one of them; a grafter.

The analyst Arjun Das, at forty-three, was a rising star in the Bureau's forensic unit. The Central Bureau of Investigations was India's FBI, with far-reaching powers that crossed state borders. Just like the FBI, it too was constantly mired by political interference.

There was stillness about him. It had earned him the nickname 'quiet analyst'. Passive by nature, in all his years of service he'd never fired a shot from his sidearm. He preferred to solve his cases through analysis, rather than in the field.

The stamp he clutched was a first issue showing Mahatma Gandhi, printed in 1966. Arjun had particular interest in the glasses worn by Gandhi on the stamp, comparing them against the ones he wore on the same stamp inside the collectors' book. Under a photograph of the stamp, it read '200 were issued in 1966; Gandhi's glasses were slightly different, then changed for later mass editions, after a disagreement. Estimated value $2500-$3500'. The stamp was a perfect match, an original. At the top end of the estimate it would cost him three months' salary. Arjun, however, was not interested in buying the stamp. There was something else about it, beyond its rarity – something worth much more and invisible to the naked eye. From his drawer he pulled a fingerprint kit. Using a soft brush, he coated the skin of the stamp with a light silver dusting. He blew off the dust specks. His finger clicked the side button on the magnifying glass, and around its inner rim, an ultraviolet light lit up.

And there it was! He grinned a cautious grin. Months of work had come down to a single fingerprint on a rare collector's stamp – a fingerprint that belonged to one S.K. Shinda. He was one of India's top five most wanted smugglers, and ran a criminal empire that dealt in black money, counterfeit goods and drugs. He had reigned unhindered for over a decade. Over this time, three separate investigations had been launched against

Shinda, but none had led to a conviction. He had powerful political friends who used their authority – and Shinda's money – to keep him out of prison. Evidence went missing, prosecution witnesses disappeared, and judges ruled out material facts. His reach seemed limitless; he seemed able to buy his way out at any price. But he hadn't met Arjun Das, the quiet analyst.

Arjun had his sights firmly set on getting Shinda this time. He was accused of ordering the killings of a respected politician, MLA V.P Banerjee, along with his wife and twin sons. Banerjee had dared to make a stand against Shinda and his political friends, pledging to make public the names of several politicians who held undeclared fortunes in foreign bank accounts filled with criminal payoffs. Banerjee's murder was particularly gruesome; he'd been decapitated. Speculation was rife that Shinda kept Banerjee's head as a trophy. It sent a clear warning to any other 'honest' politician that if they chose to take up Banerjee's stand, they could expect the same.

The rare stamp belonged to Banerjee, who was an avid collector. He'd purchased it several years earlier, but the fingerprint on the stamp wasn't his, but Shinda's. He had categorically denied ever meeting Banerjee, and stated he only knew him from media reports. The stamp was recovered during a raid on one of Shinda's known henchmen's houses. The man confessed he'd carried out the murders in a fit of rage while under the influence of drugs, but had refused to implicate Shinda in any way. The fingerprint proved otherwise.

The phone on Arjun's desk rang. He took his time to pick up, as he matched Shinda's last recorded fingerprint with the one on the stamp. He finally answered on the tenth ring, much to the annoyance of the caller.

It was from upstairs – the Assistant Director's office. Arjun was ordered to come up immediately.

Arjun asked why, but the secretary was unaccustomed to being questioned; she simply passed down the orders. This one came from the top, she repeated once more, then hung up.

Arjun placed the stamp back in a plastic pouch, put it into a secure metal box, and locked it inside his drawer. Then he left with Shinda's files in hand. A few minutes later he arrived on the top floor and headed for the door at the end of the corridor. Unlike the other doors he passed, this one had a secretary outside. She was commonly referred to as the 'control tower', as she decided who was allowed in to see the man inside – Assistant Director of the CBI, P.K. Singh. He was a mild-mannered man, a listener; he made it his business to know everyone's name, from his officers to the cleaner. When he made his monthly rounds, he made a point of greeting people by their first name. It left a personal impression, and made his staff feel he was one of them. Underneath that friendly persona, however, was a calculating bureaucrat. Like his predecessors, he'd sent officers in harm's way, and sometimes they got killed. It was part of his job.

The secretary pointed to the chair outside. Instead Arjun approached the window and peered down at the street below, where he watched the tea boy get a scolding from Raman.

'He'll see you now,' said the secretary, but before she allowed Arjun to pass, she spotted something. She pointed to his tie – or lack of one.

'I don't wear one, I—'

She wasn't impressed, but before she could say any more, Singh appeared. She got up from her chair, grabbed her pen and pad, expecting to be called in, but Singh gave her another task.

'Bring some tea. Arjun, would you like some?' said Singh, his accent more English than the English.

'No, sir, I'm fine.'

On entering Singh's office, Arjun found everything had its place, from the perfectly positioned stationery on his desk to his polished leather chair and the creaseless national flag perched between portraits of Nehru and Gandhi. Even the chair opposite his was dropped in height, making small the tallest of his guests. Singh was a pragmatist, and close to retirement. When he was first appointed to the post, he made sure senior analysts within the Bureau rose on merit, and merit alone. He sought no favours and gave none, which earned him enemies. Neither did he believe in quotas, for women or castes. That was, until now. Today he was going to break his own rule.

'Take a seat, Arjun.'

As he sat down, Arjun noticed the bold text on the memo sheet in front of Singh. Even though it was upside down, he could still make out some words: *URGENT* and *Varanasi*.

Singh browsed through a collection of photographs and then placed them in front of Arjun. They were a mix of colour and black-and-white stills, of girls.

'You're originally from Varanasi, aren't you?' Singh asked.

'Yes sir,' replied Arjun as he worked through the photographs. Nothing stood out.

'I've lived in Delhi for twenty-five years and yet I still feel like a stranger. What about you – do miss home?'

'No, sir.'

Singh wasn't convinced. He'd seen Arjun's workroom, which was furnished with things that belonged more at home than in an office.

'You don't get out much – what do they call you again? The quiet one, or something like that. Anyway, I've got something for you, to get you outside.' Singh got down to business, picking up a second stack of photographs to his side. After a brief glance at them, he gave them one by one to Arjun. These were very different. Gone were the smiles and mischief captured in the first set of photographs.

'The first girl was found three months ago. Her burned remains were discovered alongside a river on the outskirts of Varanasi.'

Singh's final word, Varanasi, caught Arjun's attention. Singh expected it.

'Two months later, it was this girl, then the next. The fourth girl's body was found three days ago. As far as we can tell, the victims were burned to death, and their remains were left in the open to be found. What do you make of it?' He passed over the victim sheets.

Arjun read through the data as the secretary entered with a single cup of tea. As she put it down, a glimpse of one of the photographs left her nauseated. She left quickly. Arjun waited until she had shut the door.

'Assuming these murders are connected and committed by the same person, then we have a clear case of a serial killer. These individuals usually share a common need to display their work, much like an artist needs an audience, sometimes for publicity, and to show off to others. Most of them want to be found, so they leave a calling card, a trail of evidence, so they can play the game.'

'A game? This is no game,' said Singh.

'It's always a game! Them and us, whatever the motive. This will only stop if – and I mean if – we find them. Otherwise the game goes on. Judging by the evidence, my guess is whoever is doing this wants to be found.'

'And I have every confidence you will find them. As of now, this is your case.'

'But sir, I'm already tied up with Shinda's case. Actually, I've had a breakthrough...' Arjun put his own files on the table, but before he could open them, Singh gave him his answer.

'Shashi's taking over. He's probably outside now. I'm sorry, but I need you on this – I want you in Varanasi by morning.' It was an order. Arjun noticed Singh's unease at cutting him off – something had forced his hand. Arjun ran through the victim sheets once more, paying more attention this time. A few things stood out. The girls were of similar age, single, and from the district of Varanasi. However, something else stood out more clearly: their surnames. Arjun read them out. 'Krishna, Das, Mistry, Ramdas... Forgive me, sir, but why did you choose me? Why not Shashi? He's more than capable.'

'It's not what you think.' Singh got defensive, and then it came: 'I know you're from the same caste as them, but I have my own reasons as well.'

Singh looked at the photo frame at the end of his desk. It held a photo of his daughter Diya. She was of a similar age to the victims. He tried to move the conversation on. 'You're not a father – you won't understand.'

Arjun didn't buy it. He kept quiet, but his silence weighed on Singh, who knew he had lost Arjun's respect.

The victims were low caste – Dalits, untouchables, part of society's underclass. Four girls among millions born into an oppressive life – not one of their making but of cultural labelling. Arjun was born with the same label. Through hard work and determination, he'd earned his rank and respect and had left Varanasi for Delhi, for a new life. Until today, Arjun felt he'd done enough.

Under pressure from the Home Office Minister, Singh had found himself on the losing end of a fight to appoint his own choice to handle the Varanasi murders. However, the Minister had wanted a Dalit officer – 'one of them', as he put it to Singh. The Minister wanted a display of action, and what better than a Dalit officer, a CBI high-flyer, a man who understood the victim's families, their communities and their pain? And if he failed, Arjun would carry the blame.

Arjun accepted, almost as if he'd read Singh's thoughts.

'Who's coming with me?' he asked.

'For now, it's just you; you'll be supported by the local force. As usual, don't expect a warm welcome. The Detective Superintendent in charge is not happy about the CBI stepping in, so be tactful.'

Singh stood up in an effort to end the conversation before Arjun asked any more questions, and led him to the door.

'Just one thing, sir – what if I fail?'

Singh gave him a stern stare – the kind you didn't reply to.

'Right,' said Arjun, and the door opened. As he stepped outside he found Shashi waiting, tie firmly in place. Arjun passed him Shinda's files. 'Yours, I believe.'

Back at his desk, Arjun filled his briefcase with case notes. He rummaged through his bottom drawer, past old staples, paperclips and worn-out pens, until he reached the far corner. Hiding in the back, he found what he was looking for: a rusty tobacco tin. The sticky residue of time and a coloured thread wrapped around the tin sealed the lid. He opened it. Inside there were a few aged photographs of a small boy and his mother, a dull silver ring, and a chunky iron key. The lock it opened fitted a door in old Assi, behind a rustic sprawl of crumbling buildings, located on the southern edge of Varanasi.

FOUR

Sunrise, District of Varanasi

A blue passenger train cut through the dawn rim, and the smell of smoky cinnamon filled the gully as a wafer-thin man, juggling a hot kettle filled to the spout with hot chai and a stack of paper cups, touted for business. Helen was still asleep. Her hand rested on a half-open book: *Following the Equator*, by Mark Twain. She'd got as far as the first few pages of Twain's commentary on his time in Varanasi. The city had moved on in many ways, sprawling beyond the colonial cantonments – districts carved out by the British Raj – but at its heart, little had changed.

Helen was woken by the enticing smells as the tea man stepped into her berth. She yawned as the tea man poured two cups – one for the elderly lady opposite Helen, and another for her middle-aged son. Perched between them was a terracotta clay pot sealed with a dark red cloth. Inside were the woman's husband's ashes: he'd been cremated the day before. The widow and her son had caught the train from Delhi. Her husband's last wish had been for his ashes to be immersed in the waters of the Ganges at Varanasi.

'We'll be arriving in Varanasi shortly,' the son said to Helen.

'That's a relief,' said Helen. Her neck was stiff from sleeping awkwardly and a day on the train.

'You're from London,' he commented. She nodded.

'Far from home.'

'What about you?' she asked.

'I'm from Delhi – Ram Prakash,' he introduced himself, and offered his business card. He was a sales agent for a paint company. She had no need of it, but took it anyway.

'You're on a business trip?' she asked.

The man's eyes moved to the urn and then to his mother, who was quietly reciting morning prayers.

'No, not this time. I'm going because of my father – he died recently.' He held the urn close.

'I'm sorry to hear that.'

'What about you – are you a tourist? I recommend a trip to Sarnath, it's not far from Varanasi.'

'Thanks, but I'm here to see my aunt. She lives in Varanasi.'

'She's also from London?'

'She left a long time ago,' said Helen as she gazed past the carriage window and out across the burning skyline, underneath which flowed endless sweeps of sugarcane fields.

FIVE

The train made its way through the fields. A farm truck waited at a crossing, the driver counting the carriages passing until the line was clear. The truck crossed over and made its way down a dusty track. Ahead, buried within the stalks, was an isolated barn. When he arrived, the young driver stepped out and went to the back. There was something moving beneath the cover, and it stopped as the man unhinged the hooks. In a single swoop he pulled off the cover and there she was – a young girl stunned with fear. Like the others, she was bound.

He picked her up and carried her into the barn. Dimly lit with a few shafts of light, the air was foul with the rotting flesh of sugarcane stalks stacked inside. He dumped her on a pile and went out to the truck to get his bag. She didn't have long. Rolling around, she looked for a way out – and found one a little distance away. An oil drum leaned against the wooden slats. Above it, a small opening was covered loosely by a cloth. She didn't know how big it was. The cloth flapped in the breeze. It was worth a try, she thought. Face down, she thrust herself towards the barrel until she reached it. Her back against the drum, she rubbed her bound hands fiercely against its rough rim until the rope split and broke free. Relieved, she climbed up and pulled off the cloth. A blast of light came into the barn. The hole was big enough for her to crawl through. She looked back at the barn door; he was still outside. She took her chance and climbed through, falling onto the dirt outside. He heard her fall and came inside. He climbed onto the barrel and looked through the hole. She was running away, fighting her way through the crops. He came after her, following the rustle as she ran, and the broken crops she left in her path. He closed in on her. She cried out, but no one heard. A few hundred metres in front of her was the road. A truck made its way down the empty lane, loaded with giant hives of sugarcane, so large they hung over both sides of the lorry. The radio was on, the driver singing along to the lyrics, bopping his head from left to right.

The girl heard the truck's approach and raised her hands high to attract the driver's attention, but the crops were higher. The man chasing her picked up his pace and closed the gap – finally he saw her. The girl came within a metre of the road. The truck approached, the driver still oblivious to her cries. She was about to break through – but then a knife stung her from behind. She stopped, and stood in silence, in pain, as she watched, through the last line of stalks, the truck pass by.

She fell as her legs gave way beneath her. With what little life she had left, she crawled through the dirt, clutching at the roots, pulling herself inch by inch until her head came through the crops and she could see the road. She gasped and rested her cheek on the dirt, her eyes barely open, and watched the truck disappear from sight. Her life was fading; her strength waned. From behind, he yanked her back into the crops. The crops folded behind her, the road was empty, and the unsettled fields were silent again.

SIX

Varanasi

The train driver signalled his arrival with a blast of his horn, long and loud, as the carriages crawled through the iron bridge. Helen got her first glimpse of the Ganges below, as the sound of conches flooded the carriages. The train was packed with hundreds of pilgrims, all with the desire to bathe in the sacred waters of the Ganges so they could purify their souls. No other place on earth meant more to Hindus than Varanasi. In life and in death, the Ganges in Varanasi offered salvation. Among them, a joyous young girl, cried out her Lord's name. The sleeper train from New Delhi came alive as it arrived in the city of Varanasi.

Even before the train had stopped, dozens of coolies, baggage men robed in red and white, thronged the platform. They crowded round the carriage doors as passengers gathered to step off even before the train had stopped. Passengers flooded the platform. In the mass of moving bodies, Helen lost hold of her bags. A coolie called out to her.

'Miss... Miss?' He gestured to her to follow him. He had her bags in either hand as well as another bundle on his head; it belonged to another passenger. The rush and noise was brought to a sudden halt by a collective gasp. The crowd leaned over the platform on the other side. Ram Prakash was on the rail track, holding his mother's head. She'd fallen, a victim of the pilgrims who had flooded the platform and pushed the frail old lady off the platform's edge. Her son looked up at the silent crowd as blood trickled from under her hair and pooled in his palms.

'Maa, Maa... Maa,' he cried out, but his mother was gone.

Helen stopped and watched from the footbridge, but then the coolie tugged her to move on.

'Come, madam.'

'The old lady – she's hurt,' said Helen.

'She's expired – gone,' he said with a casual wave, barely taking the time to look at her. 'Don't worry, madam; it was her destiny.' The coolie walked on, mumbling to the other passenger, who was also rushing: 'Blessed are those who die in Banaras' (Varanasi).

SEVEN

Behind the barn, there was a group of old banyan trees. Beneath one a fresh mound of soil grew around a ditch. The digger wiped sweat from his forehead and sank his shovel into the dirt. He took the lifeless girl by her feet and dragged her into the ditch. He shovelled the soil over her, leaving her face until last. He rested beside her, looking into her glazed eyes. It wasn't supposed to end this way – he was angry. Her death was a worthless sacrifice. He leaned over and closed her eyes, his fingers passing down her cold skin to her lips. He opened her mouth and placed something inside it. He then finished shovelling the dirt over her, and left the grave.

EIGHT

Kapil Dhara, Varanasi

A black-and-yellow rickshaw was parked at the edge of an uneven track. A cyclist passed it, his cycle wheels bouncing over the rubble as he rode through the village of Kapil Dhara, located east of the main city and on the verge of the Varuna River. The village was small and surrounded by trees and woodland. As well as a small Hindu temple, the village was home to a mission. Housed within a sandstone building, the thick wooden doors sat beneath a fading hand-painted sign, tilted off-centre, that read *ST XAVIER'S MISSION*. The mission was run by a small group of sisters. They also ran an orphanage, which provided refuge and an education for its young residents. The orphanage was filled with the dispossessed; children of any faith, and of none.

In the rear passenger seat, Helen waited as the driver slouched to one side, catching up on his sleep. He'd left the radio on, tuned to the local news; the headline was the tragic story of the old lady's death at the railway station. The village milkman walked up to the mission door, a bowed bamboo cane resting across his shoulders, weighed down on either side by fresh pots of goat's milk. He announced his arrival.

'Ramu-doodwala' – the milkman is here. A few moments later the front door opened and he disappeared inside. It was now Helen's turn. She tapped the driver's shoulder and paid him off. Bags in hand, she arrived at the front door, which was open. She perked up and stepped inside, anxious about meeting her aunt. Helen's only memory of her was from her mother's stories and photographs.

Once inside, she found herself in a small courtyard, an oasis of plants and flowerbeds, far removed from the dust outside. A young girl, no more than seven, strolled around with a baby goat, and another young girl appeared from under the arches with a bucket of water. Helen watched her disappear behind a large stone planter, then a voice from behind her greeted the girl. It was Aunt Agatha. With the girl, she poured water into the planter and flowerpots below. She stopped as Helen's shadow cast over her. She put down the bucket and turned to Helen. Helen's warm smile froze as she faced her.

'Can I help you?' asked Agatha, curiosity in her voice. 'Who are you?'

Helen, barely a foot away, was shocked by the reappearance of her mother's face, but it wasn't Sarah – it was Agatha, her mother's twin. The two were identical in every way: they had the same pale skin, blonde hair, blue eyes and build. Agatha wore her hair in a ponytail, unlike Sarah, who had worn hers straight. Helen had always known her mother had a twin, but to see her face to face so soon after Sarah's death left her speechless. Agatha repeated her question, and finally Helen answered.

'Helen,' she said. 'I'm Helen… Sarah's daughter.'

Agatha gulped, and for a moment appeared lost. Her eyes closed as she gathered her thoughts.

'Helen,' gasped Agatha under her breath. 'Helen.' She noticed the pendant around Helen's neck, and any doubts quickly faded. Her guarded surprise turned to warmth as she embraced her. Helen felt awkward at first, but Agatha's arms held her firmly – she'd waited so long to hold her. Helen, the daughter she had left behind.

Under the morning sun, the two of them sat beneath the veranda, side by side, mother and daughter, secrets between them. A gentle wind breezed through the courtyard, lifting the flower petals. The broken ones danced in the air. Helen broke the news of Sarah's death. Agatha sat, numb at first. Tears swelled and hung from her lashes; she was too reserved to show her grief, even to Helen.

'I can't remember the last time I spoke to her,' said Agatha. 'To take her own life – she must have felt so alone.' She held Helen's hand. 'I should have been there for her, for you both.' Her head sank in shame.

'She often spoke of you, her sister the missionary – she was so proud of you.' Helen unclipped the pendant from her neck and put it into Agatha's hand.

'She left a letter for me.' Helen paused. 'She wanted me to come here, to you, to bring you this. She didn't say why, just that you would understand. What did she mean by that?'

'I… I don't know,' said Agatha, unable, or unwilling, to confront her past. Helen was here now and that was all that mattered: in time she would find a way to tell her. Agatha moved aside the collar of her top to reveal her own identical pendant, and took it off, placing it next to Sarah's.

'They belonged to your grandmother, and hers before. Your great-grandfather bought them from a silversmith when he was stationed in Varanasi. He was a medical officer in the British Army. He always talked about his time here, especially of his time on the ghats. He filled me with ideas. The same ones that brought me here in the end.'

'They look beautiful together – what are they?' Helen asked.

'Tulsi,' replied Agatha. 'Let me show you; come with me.' Agatha walked over to the stone planter at the centre of the courtyard. It was a relic left by the original owners of the building. The planter was overflowing with Tulsi – lush green delicate threads with scented leaves branching out in every direction. Agatha held a stem and gently broke off a small Tulsi leaf. After taking in its scent, she passed it to Helen.

'Tulsi's been growing here for over two centuries. Somehow it has managed to survive all the changes: it's an ancient Hindu symbol of an eternal bond.'

Agatha took Helen's hand and returned Sarah's pendant.

'You should have it – it was what she wanted,' said Helen.

'Dear child, it's not about the pendant, it's about you. Sarah found a way to bring you here.'

NINE

Agatha guided Helen into a small room. It was simple, with a half-broken fan blade dangling above a hanging bed. Apart from a few dusty books stacked on a shelf, an grubby oil lantern and a side chair, the room was bare.

'It's not much, I'm afraid. I'll have it cleaned up for you,' said Agatha as she dusted down the bed with a rag. 'You are staying – you must.'

'I wouldn't have it any other way, and as for the room, it's more than I expected, Aunt Agatha.' Helen sat down on the swinging bed; it creaked as the rope stretched from under the ceiling.

'I'll arrange for some bath water to be brought inside, so you can freshen up and rest. I'll come back for you later.'

'Aunt Agatha, I—' Helen stuttered as she suddenly felt Sarah's absence.

'I miss her too.'

Agatha left, closing the door. She paused briefly on the either side. Holding her pendant, she whispered, 'Forgive me, forgive me.'

Helen lay down on the bed. A lack of sleep weighed her down. She reached out to the switch and flicked it on. The single fan blade spun slowly. She followed its curling path until her eyes tired, and soon after she fell asleep.

Inside the mission chapel, lit only by a handful of candles, on her knees, in front of the glazed wooden Christ, Agatha prayed for her sister's soul, as Sarah had committed the ultimate sin by taking her own life. But another sin, not of Sarah's making, had robbed Helen of her childhood.

Helen tossed from side to side as the past invaded her sleep. In sleep, sweating from fear, troubling voices filled her dreams.

'No,' she said. 'No, leave me alone!' She heard a thump against the door. Her eyes flickered. As the thumps grew louder, she turned. 'No, please no!' She heard a child weeping in fear, and she covered her ears with her hands, but the thumping continued.

'No,' she cried out and with a final gasp, Helen was awake. The fan stopped spinning. She gathered her breath. Her top clung sweatily to her skin.

TEN

Midday, Varanasi

An old-fashioned grey Mahindra police jeep made its way through the sprawling traffic, cattle, cycles, rickshaws and pedestrians, as they crossed the mighty Malviya iron bridge that spanned the Ganges below, at the other end of the old city of Varanasi.

Halfway across, Arjun asked the constable to pull over. He stepped out, onto the footpath, and leaned over the rails in front of him. He watched a loaded barge, full of wood, head in the direction of the burning ghats. He was home. He puffed on his cigarette a final time and retreated into the jeep. Arjun sat quietly as the jeep moved on, looking through the grilled bars on the side windows as they crossed the river. Not much had changed inside the old city, but around its edges shapeless buildings were under construction as the city expanded.

'First time in Varanasi?' the constable asked, looking at Arjun through the mirror. He was met with silence. Arjun had kept quiet, saying nothing throughout the journey from the airport to the city; lost in his thoughts. As they passed through the old city, he reflected on his views of familiar temples and children playing in streets. Arjun pushed his fingers through the window bars, reaching out to the world outside, wanting to touch it, to feel it and be part of it. The same world that had been far out of his reach when he was a child.

The police jeep pulled off the highway and entered the district police station. Its tree-lined lawn was neatly trimmed, the building a whitewashed relic of the British Raj. Once an administrative powerhouse of Englishmen, it was now home to a small army of police officers in khaki uniforms. The officers lacked formality and the sharpness of their counterparts in New Delhi. This was Varanasi, India's Wild West, where disputes were settled at the barrel of a gun. It bred its own kind of police officer, and outsiders were unwelcome.

Arjun stepped inside, escorted by a senior officer. The two walked down the central corridor. On both sides, open doors gave him glimpses of officers at work, and piles of blue files, stacked head-high. Giant fans hummed above, blades turning slowly, not fast enough to cool the sweating officers below. A rounded officer sat in the corner, his shirt undone, showing his chest, his chin dripping sweat. He jumped out of his chair when Arjun and the senior officer peered in; all the policemen did. In the fuss, the rounded officer struggled to hold up his unbuckled trousers while standing to attention, much to Arjun's amusement.

Finally, Arjun arrived outside Deputy Superintendent of Police Mehra's office. He was offered a seat by Mehra's staff officer, who was perched at a small desk outside the door, but Arjun chose to stand. The officer knocked and went in. Mehra was on the receiving end of an unwelcome phone call from the political office of the local Member of Parliament. He was being ordered to co-operate with New Delhi's man and swiftly bring the killer to justice. After the call ended, the senior officer announced Arjun's arrival. Already agitated, Mehra was in no hurry to see him straight away. Instead he sent for another officer, Rajveer Saxsena.

Arjun waited, pacing up and down, taking short steps, occasionally noting the time. For the first twenty minutes, he made no fuss, but after an hour Arjun's frustration was visible. There was no sign of Saxsena either. He asked the junior officer outside Mehra's door how much longer he would be, but the officer had no idea and he wasn't about to ask either.

Then Saxsena appeared from behind them.

'Excuse me,' she said. Arjun he stepped aside and watched her walk into Mehra's office. Arjun found the door closed firmly behind her.

'This is ridiculous. It's been over an hour – I insist on seeing him now,' he demanded.

The junior officer waiting with him refused.

'Right then, I'll do it myself.' Arjun reached out for the door handle, just as the door was opened from the inside.

'Mr Das?' Saxsena asked as she let him in.

DSP Mehra was an old-school police chief, full of bravado, heavy in weight, with an inflated notion of his own importance. As far as Mehra was concerned, this was his city, his officers, and he ruled them both on his own terms. He'd never seen New Delhi, or any other major Indian city. For Mehra, life began in Varanasi – and as far as he was concerned, his would end there.

Arjun took the chair next to Saxsena, who sat quietly. She'd received Mehra's message over an hour ago, when he'd told her to come to his office in an hour's time. He had deliberately kept Arjun waiting, sending a clear message to his guest from Delhi that he would continue to do things in his own way and in his own time. He read the first page sheet of Arjun's profile – not that he needed to; he'd read it several times over.

'I see you were born here, in Varanasi. So was I,' said Mehra. 'So you'll have an understanding of how things work around here. This is not Delhi; you won't see any fast police cars and fancy police towers here. We may be a bit old-fashioned, but my officers work just as hard. We keep our noses clean and do what we can. But some people think that's not good enough, and that why you're here, to shake things up, isn't it?'

Arjun kept quiet and didn't take the bait. Mehra was looking for a confrontation, anything to provoke him, to put him on the back foot.

He ranted on. 'I don't like being told how to run my business, not by Delhi and not by you. Whatever you've been told, forget it – are you clear?'

'Yes,' said Arjun in a submissive tone.

'Yes, sir!' demanded Mehra.

'Do you have any idea how many girls go missing here every week? We don't have the manpower of Delhi, but we do our best.' The district had a high number of missing girl cases, largely due to its conservative nature: girls eloped with their boyfriends to avoid forced marriages within their castes.

Mehra lowered his voice as he turned to his latest appointment.

'I've already replaced the senior case officer. Saxsena's now in charge, and she's very capable. I suggest you assist her where you can – after all, you're here to co-operate with us, right?'

Arjun pulled out his appointment letter and extended it to Mehra. He wasn't there to play second fiddle; he was there to lead the case.

'But sir,' Arjun said. 'I've written authority from Delhi to—'

He was cut off by Mehra.

'Written authority! Delhi doesn't run things around here – I do, and don't forget it!'

A resolute Arjun folded the letter and played his last hand. He glanced at his watch, then stood, picking up his coat and bag.

'As you wish, sir. Please excuse me; I have a flight to catch back to Delhi.' Arjun made his way to the door.

It was Mehra's call. His thumb flashed red as he pressed hard on his pen.

'Wait, sit down, sit down,' said Mehra. He folded. Arjun sat down again as Saxsena sat by, a quiet spectator.

'Fine – do it your way, but make one mistake and Saxsena takes over. If you don't like it, go back to Delhi.'

ELEVEN

Arjun followed Saxsena into the special investigations unit, located at the end of the main building. It was more of an outpost, with half a dozen officers parked inside, tapping away on their typewriters. Saxsena's office was tucked away in the back. There were no walls around her space; just an informal stack of files separated her from her officers. She was lucky to have a window and a view, even though it was just of the rear yard, and the only computer in the office. Arjun looked around. He had his work cut out, he thought. As he stepped into Saxsena's space, he found the floor carpeted by layers of files, many still tied with string. He looked around for a desk but Saxsena had other plans.

'Tripathi!' She summoned her junior officer. Tripathi came inside. He was the most promising among her team, she thought, the rest of whom had been passed down from other units: dead wood as far as she was concerned, but she had to work with what she had.

'Prepare a desk and some stationery,' she said as she pointed to the corner outside.

'Ah, wait one minute…' Arjun grabbed some boxes from the side table and passed them to Tripathi, who turned to Saxsena with a puzzled look, which disappeared as another stack of files were loaded up. Arjun steered Tripathi through the file walls.

'I'm sure you'll find somewhere to put them down.'

'This will do just fine.' Arjun dumped his bag on top of a table and found a chair to sit on. He cleared the floor underneath his feet and found an old photo frame stashed between loose papers.

'I hope you don't mind, seeing we're working together.'

Saxsena kept quiet. Arjun held on to the photo frame. Under the glass was a black-and-white photograph of a middle-aged man and woman, wearing awkward smiles, not looking used to having their picture taken.

'By the way,' he started, but before he could finish Saxsena snatched the frame from him. He took a chance and grabbed her wrist.

'A family photo?' he asked, staring at her and observing her reactions. He found her pulse; a second later he let her go. She didn't take kindly him touching her, and returned behind her desk. She placed the photo frame in her drawer and slammed it shut. In the seconds he had held her wrist, he had felt her racing pulse and watched her pupils dilate. She didn't like his question; she was hiding something.

'Do you mind if I call you by your first name?' he asked.

'Sure,' she replied, picking up a pen and pad, ready to proceed with his instructions.

'And I prefer Arjun – it's less formal. So, Rajveer, where are you from?'

'What do you mean?'

'Where is your home? Judging by your accent, you're not local. If I was to make a guess, I'd say Punjab, North Punjab, a border town perhaps? Judging by your demeanour, a military connection? I'm right, aren't I?' Arjun insisted.

'That's one of your party tricks.' Rajveer was impressed. 'I'm from Firozpur, twenty kilometres from the Pakistan border. My father served in the border protection force.'

'Firozpur,' said Arjun, as he slapped his hand on the table, pleased he had got it right. 'I'm sorry for the intrusion – it's just a game, and I usually get it wrong most of the time.' But he was lying; he didn't believe her. He'd made it up and she'd bought in to his suggestion. He decided he'd wait until another time to figure out why.

'So now you're in charge, where do you want to start?' Rajveer asked.

'The case files,' Arjun replied.

She pointed to them: on the floor, on the windowsill, piled in the stacks outside – they were everywhere.

TWELVE

Afternoon, the Mission

Inside her room, Agatha flicked through a collection of old photographs – of her childhood with Sarah, and the two of them back in London. Among them was a photograph of Helen, barely a week old, cradled in her palms. She let her tears run free as her past caught up with her.

Across the courtyard, Helen lay, face up, in a large tin tub, a relic from the time the mission was used as a British military hospital. Her thin frame sank into it on one side, with her knees popping out from the water at the other end. Occasionally her mouth breached the water's skin for air. The water rippled every ten seconds as a droplet fell from a hanging pipe. Helen held her breath as the drip created a new ripple, but this time she stayed under, holding her breath, staring, cocooned in the water. Her sight blurred, and she felt a thump under another ripple. She kept holding her breath. In the haze, she dreamed that a heavy fist pounded on the door; she imagined the forced turn of the handle; she heard her name being called. She kept still as another ripple pierced the sheen. Without air, her flesh lost its colour. She was held under by the same dreams that had stolen her sleep. She was ready to surrender; to end her dreams and fall into an eternal sleep. Her last breath escaped her lips and bubbled to the surface as her eyes shut.

'Helen... Helen,' said Agatha as she tapped against the door. She raised her voice and tried harder, peering through the window bars, but there was no sign of Helen in the room.

'Helen… Helen!' She banged hard on the door. Helen's eyes popped open as she heard Agatha's plea.

'Uh,' she gasped as she exploded from under the water, clutching the tub. Her lungs sucked in air; her skin shivered; her head rested on the rim.

'Helen, Helen… are you OK?' Agatha grew anxious when she did not reply.

'I'm fine, Aunt Agatha… just fine.'

THIRTEEN

Late Afternoon, Ghats of Varanasi

As the sun bled across the skyline, the sandstone walls of the old city bronzed in the heat. A rickshaw weaved its way through the narrow roads until the path was too narrow to pass.

'Where are we going?' Helen asked as she stepped out of the rickshaw.

'A boat ride,' replied Agatha. They made the short journey through the maze of buildings, intoxicating sights and smells all around them. Each turn brought them past another temple or an idol etched on a wall. Worshippers of all ages trailed past, and the sounds of Sanskrit chanting grew louder.

'*Ram name satya ha!*' (Lord Ram is truth) cried out the leader of a funeral procession, his followers repeating the same words over and over. They carried a corpse wrapped in red cloth in the direction of the river. Helen let them pass. As the river neared, she felt its breeze and on the next turn she saw it. The mighty Ganges filled her sight. A swarm of foreign tourists brushed past her as they tried to keep up with their local guide. He gathered his flock on the steps and took off his sandals; they did the same. He then stepped into the river. The cool water washed over his feet, and he encouraged the tourists to join him. He extended his arm to an elderly American, and helped him in by his side. A dozen or more chattering tourists found their tongues silenced as the mother of all rivers greeted them with her blessing. Agatha made room for Helen to watch as the tourist guide performed his miracle. He took out a pocket knife and held the blade to his fingertip. He said a small prayer, then made a cut in his finger. The tourists nearest to him cringed as he pressed on the cut and forced a dribble of blood to seep out. He was all smiles, and made sure everyone in his group saw his wound. He then dipped his finger into the river and prayed to Ganga, the river goddess, to heal his wound.

'You'll see – this time tomorrow it will be healed,' he declared with full confidence. His fingertip was still scarred by previous cuts, but he was too smart to allow anyone to see that.

The American joked, 'You'd better get that seen to. The water's filthy: you'll catch an infection.'

'No sir, you are wrong,' replied the guide. 'Look around you, sir. While *you* may not believe, there are thousands here who do. They see what you do not, and believe in what you do not. I am sure, one day, when you are back home, you will remember this day and, for a passing moment, you will believe – just like me, just like them.'

'Do you believe in what he said?' Helen asked Agatha.

'Yes, I do,' she replied with conviction. 'We can all conjure up miracles, that's the easy part. It's believing in something more, without miracles or proof, that forges one's faith. These pilgrims believe in this place; they haven't come here in search of miracles. They've come here because they have faith: this is the centre of their universe.'

'And what about you?' Helen asked.

'It's my heart – everything.'

FOURTEEN

Ganges, Varanasi

Away from the buzz and shuffle of the ghats, a narrow longboat coasted along the sleepy waters of the Ganges. The man rowing it held the boat steady as it glided past the sinking sandstone steps and muddy sandbanks. Sitting on the backless hard bench at the other end, Helen asked Agatha, 'How old is this place?' as she raised her camera.

'Some say it's as old as time,' replied Agatha. 'I'd like to believe that was true.'

They passed a mass of pilgrims bathing in the river, cleansing their souls of sin. Helen snapped and zoomed in. Faces appeared in the frame, young and old – true believers. A gang of local boys plunged into the waters, diving and spinning as they pleased, vanishing beneath the water and reappearing to applause. Helen joined in with the applause. The boys waved back at her, playing to her camera. She waved back and took some snaps as the boat moved along.

'It's a special place for Hindus – and for me. There's a sense of faith here, so strong that it goes beyond religion. It's raw and truthful in nature,' said Agatha.

'I know that man,' said Helen suddenly, peering through the viewfinder. In her sights was Ram Prakash from the train. He wore a white loincloth, and his face looked lost as he surrendered to the priest's instruction.

'He's performing the last rites,' said Agatha. 'See the urns by his side? He'll release the ashes into the Ganges at the end of the ceremony. It must have been someone close to him.'

The oarsman steered the longboat closer to the riverbank. The sheen of the water dulled a little, and wilted flower petals and flakes of ash washed back and forth along the shoreline. Above the murky water, several pyres were still alight. Their boat was about to be penned in as several longboats closed in on them, each filled to the brim with eager tourists competing to capture a shot of the pyres.

Behind the fires, above the steps, someone took an interest in Helen. He was sitting in the shade of a steep stairwell. Raising his camera, the young man zoomed in until he had Helen's face in focus. As she looked across at the pyres, she remembered her mother. He clicked the shutter, capturing her grief. Helen put her camera down. She felt uncomfortable intruding on a stranger's grief. She asked the oarsman to move away.

The boat settled back to a gentle pace down the centre of the river, and a marigold flower floated into reach. Helen leaned out and swooped it up. She held it briefly. Its fragrance still strong. She then returned it to the river so it could continue its journey.

Agatha noticed Helen's mood change. She was less inquisitive and quiet.

'Look over there,' said Agatha, pointing to the setting sun. Helen turned to the horizon while Agatha watched her.

'So beautiful,' Agatha whispered.

FIFTEEN

Sunset, Old City, Varanasi

BEEP... BEEP, the horn bleated. The police jeep was stuck, sandwiched between a thin alley and two bullocks which blocked its path as they grazed, unconcerned, on scraps. *BEEP... BEEP*. The driver tried to hurry them on, but these were Banarasi bullocks – stubborn and tough, they stood their ground. The driver threw up his hands in frustration.

'I'll be fine from here,' said Arjun. He stepped out with his bag and case and squeezed past the two bullocks. He turned a corner, passed through a small lightless tunnel, emerged on the other side and climbed the steps. The sidewalls were painted in turquoise. At the end he arrived at a heavy door marked by red paste covering a small carving of Lord Hanuman, the monkey king. The door was half open. Arjun stepped inside. An aged banyan tree overhung the small courtyard, its roots merging into the stonework, and its branches providing modest shade. Arjun walked under the tree as the leaves bristled, thanks to a monkey scrabbling through the branches. He remembered his childhood in the same spot. While the tree had aged a little, the mischief of the monkeys was still the same. He threw up an apple for the monkey, an entrance fee that granted him passage. He walked along the terrace, passing the first and second doors until he arrived at the last one, which was sealed with a rusty lock. Arjun took the key from around his neck and slotted it in the keyhole. It needed a shake to break the crust of dirt and rust in it before he managed to open it. When he pushed back the door, he was greeted by years of dust and cobwebs. The room was dark and filled with choking air.

He stepped inside, leaving footprints trailing behind, imprints in the thick dust. He looked around the room he had been born in, lived in and which his parents died in. The flameless oil lamp hanging on a nail was empty. He flicked open his lighter and followed the flame around the walls until he saw his father's photograph on the wall. He stepped closer as the flame flickered across his father's eyes. Arjun, aged seven, recalled his father's words as he returned from a scuffle with other boys, who taunted him because of his caste.

'Why do they treat me differently?' Arjun had asked.

'They're just uneducated boys. Never let them bother you, Arjun. When I was your age, I asked my father the same question, and do you want to know what he told me?'

'Yes, Papa.'

'He said a great man once said that God never made man to consider another man as untouchable.'

'Did he tell you who said that, Papa?' asked Arjun.

'Yes, he did, Arjun... Mahatma Gandhi'

Arjun wiped the dust from the frame. He coughed and covered his mouth; the air needing clearing. He went up to the rear wooden window and pushed it open. A welcome wind swept in and, along with a flush of evening light, beyond the buildings ahead, he found the view he had missed the most: a glimpse of the shimmering waters of the Ganges, painted orange by the sunset.

SIXTEEN

Night, Old City, Varanasi

Longboats congregated in front of Dashashwamedh, the most venerated of all the ghats. One hundred and more boats, both small and large, jolted up and down as the tourists on board jostled for the best positions to watch the evening puja, or worship. To find a better view, Agatha took Helen from boat to boat until they found the steps. They sat among the locals as a line of priests lit a spiral of candles. Thousands gathered on all sides as the priests performed the Ganga Prayers. After it was over, they walked along the footpath that ran parallel with the riverbank, leaving behind the bright lights and crowds.

Helen was drawn to the remains of a funeral pyre burning on the edge of the sandbanks. In the darkness, a naked man stood out. He was covered with silver ash and sat in a trance. Agatha walked a few steps ahead, unaware that Helen had stopped. The man broke his trance and found Helen staring at him. His sunken eyes and silver flesh were ghostly in appearance. As she stood, frozen, he took ash from the funeral pyre and threw it over his head. Looking up, he welcomed it as it fell upon his face.

'Helen,' Agatha called her, realising she'd stopped. When she failed to respond, Agatha went to fetch her. She saw the man covered in ash and saw how Helen was fascinated by him.

'Helen, Helen, let's move on.' Agatha held her hand and tugged her away.

'I'm sorry, I… just couldn't move. I don't know why, I just froze.'

'Did you see what he did?' Helen asked.

'Yes, I did, but don't let it frighten you; he's harmless. Some of the things you'll see here need a lifetime to understand.'

Further along the footpath, Arjun sat on the steps, soaking up the silence. He lit a cigarette and watched the river dwellers light their lanterns, stacked high on stilts besides their boats. The river, thick and black, was all but hidden; occasionally it sparkled in the passing moonlight.

Agatha recognised an old friend.

'Arjun,' she said as she stepped down to his side.

'Agatha,' he said with surprise.

'It is you,' said Agatha. He was no longer the young man she had known, but his eyes, although they were a little tired, were still the same.

'When did you get back?' she asked.

'Today.'

'It's so good to see you.' She introduced Helen.

'This is…' She paused until she found the right words. 'My niece Helen. She also arrived today, from London.'

'First time in Varanasi?' Arjun asked.

'It's my first time in India,' Helen replied.

'I'm sure Agatha will show you around. The best way to experience this place is to embrace it – isn't that right, Agatha?'

She agreed.

'I'll bear that in mind,' said Helen.

'Are you still living in Delhi or staying this time?' Agatha asked Arjun.

'Still in Delhi, although I must admit I do miss this place from time to time. I'm staying at my father's place for now.'

'Your parents would have been so proud. I expect to see you at the mission when you have time.'

'I've some work to do, but I'll definitely pass by when I have the time. It will be great to see everyone again.'

Arjun had first met Agatha as a teenager when he visited the mission's chapel with his parents. His father had helped to build the orphanage, not far from his own village. Arjun's parents, like other Dalits, found the temple doors of the old city off-limits, as the priests shunned them, fearing their presence would pollute their hallowed ground. In contrast, Agatha welcomed them to the mission's chapel, where they were free to pray to their own gods.

SEVENTEEN

It was late evening when Arjun arrived at the district police station. He found it largely empty, apart from two officers at reception who were busy watching a television show, and a cleaner washing the floor. Arjun walked past all of them without speaking.

Inside the back office, Arjun emptied out an oily bag of freshly cooked samosas onto a plate. He nibbled at one as he turned the desk lamp on. He looked around the chaotic splash of files and papers, and decided it was time to put things in order. He spent the first hour tidying up, briefly flicking through each file before assigning it to a pile. At the end, he had one large stack of useless files and a small stack of relevant files. He worried he would find little of value in the files.

As the midnight hour passed, the last train of the day went by, on its way to Delhi. As well as the clock ticking, he could make out the churns and clunks of the train wheels riding over the rails. The samosas were gone and his cigarette packet was empty. He had found nothing of interest in the files. As he snapped the last file shut, he noticed the cover. The white label was clean, but underneath that he made out the faint print of a stamp. He read the words *PENDING/CLOSED*, and he speculated whether the file cover had had a previous life. He picked up the phone to find out. No one answered; the ringing was buried under the sound of the television show. It rang a few more times. Arjun was about to hang up when the show cut to a commercial. Finally the reception officer heard the phone and answered.

'Hello, sir.'

'Tell me – I have a file marked *PENDING/CLOSED*. What does that mean?' Arjun asked.

The reception officer tried to find the words to explain it. 'Sir, that file is… how do you say? Closed, but not closed… I mean, it's, what do you say...'

'It's unresolved?' Arjun interjected.

'Yes sir – unresolved. Not closed but not solved.' It sounded like a bad joke, but it wasn't. Given the mess he'd found, nothing surprised him.

'Where can I find these files?

'In the basement… Hello sir? Sir?'

But there was no answer. By the time the reception officer dialled back, Arjun had arrived at his desk. He asked the officer to take him to the basement; he followed with a set of keys and a torch. The door was unlocked, but still needed force to open it. As the two pushed through it, the officer grabbed Arjun before he fell down the steep steps just beyond the door. There were three light switches to one side. None of them worked. The officer flicked his torch on and shone it on the steps.

'Thanks, I'll take it from here,' said Arjun as he took the torch from the officer.

He made his way along the racks of files, dusting down the labels marked on the front of each box. Most were scribbled on, the words illegible. He moved on. He decided to go to the far end and work his way back; it was more likely older files would be kept there. His hunch paid off: a stack of boxes appeared in the torchlight, and he found the two words he was looking for: *OPEN/PENDING*. There were too many boxes for him to carry. Each was crammed with thirty or more files, their edges rough from age. He pulled out one to check. The front was marked *OPEN/PENDING,* just like the one upstairs. He glanced inside, and quickly made out the case: the abduction of two girls, the first aged nine and the second seven. They'd been reported missing after failing to return home from school. The boxes were filled with similar cases – missing faces, like the files, never to be seen again. The administration officer received an allowance to purchase new files, but he often found it to his advantage to empty an old box of its files and reuse them for new cases. He pocketed the money he didn't have to spend on new files, which was a few hundred rupees at best. It didn't bother him that the files were emptied of their paperwork, and with them the cases. They were gathering dust in the basement where no one visited. They were forgotten.

Arjun was nothing if not thorough. If the answers were not upstairs, then he had to dig deeper, to older cases, in the basement where no one else had bothered to look. He knew from experience that sometimes history provided the best clues. Serial killers were known to play a long game, holding a deep-rooted grudge or desire for vengeance. Arjun had no idea which it was, but he had been sent in to do what the local force hadn't: look for answers in unexpected places.

'Hello! Hello?' Arjun shouted from the stairs. His voice echoed down the corridor. Moments later the reception officer arrived, and Arjun passed him three boxes. He took another three himself and together they returned to the office. He noted the time as he waded through each file – 3.35am. The stack worth a second look still remained thin.

His neck ached, his eyes burned, as the light outside lifted. Dawn arrived with a call for prayer, echoing from the city's minarets. He picked up the second-last file, and browsed past the first page. It was a suicide case – he'd seen several of the same. He turned a page and found a newspaper clipping. At the centre of the article was a photograph of a woman – a young bride.

EIGHTEEN

Police Station, Varanasi

Rajveer was the last to arrive that morning. When she walked in, she found the lights were off and the window shut. In the darkness, her team of officers watched a slide show projected on the wall. Standing beside the slide machine, the air thick with the smoky scent of burning dust, Arjun pointed to the projected map. The map projected across his face and chest. Standing at the back of the room, Rajveer peered through the stacks of files to her office. She noticed the floor was clear of papers, and she saw the tidy stack of files on Arjun's desk.

'You're just in time,' Arjun remarked as he saw Rajveer standing there.

He'd prepared a pep talk to energise the officers. The version he presented was tamed; his earlier drafts had been more scolding. The case had been mishandled from the start, when the first girl had been reported missing. There was a clear lack of immediate action and follow-through as the body count mounted, and Mehra, for his part, had provided the bare minimum of resources. A Bollywood film star visiting the ghats for a film shoot was given more police resources and Mehta's personal attention than the initial murders. Arjun was determined to move the officers on and take them with him; dwelling on lost opportunities would do nothing to catch the killer. So he tactfully sidestepped past performance and focused instead on what needed to be done from now on. He started with a recap and a reminder of what was at stake.

The slide moved on to a photograph of the first victim. She had a gentle, shy face. The camera had captured her subtle smile. Arjun flicked to the next slide, and the second victim appeared.

'Reena, Hena, Meera and Devika.' Arjun read out the girls' names as the slides changed.

'Wonderful young girls, in the prime of their lives. With everything to look forward to – someone's sister, someone's daughter.'

The slides changed to show each victim's remains. The officers' stomachs churned as they confronted the sickening sight of a charred corpse, curled and deformed and scarred by tar.

'Look at them now. Whoever did this burned these girls alive.

Rajveer squinted as she was confronted with a close-up of a burned face.

'I know you've all given your best and worked hard on these, but it's not enough; we need to work harder. That's why I am here – to push you to dig deeper and to re-examine the facts. Together we'll catch this monster. I want every lead, every statement re-checked. I want to know what each of these girls were doing in the days and weeks before they were murdered. I want you to find out who their friends were, who their boyfriends were, where they hung out. There's always a connection.'

Arjun stubbed out his cigarette and turned the projector off. He followed Rajveer into the back office, where she lifted the blind.

'I see you've been busy,' Rajveer said. She flicked through the nearest stack of files. She recognised the covers from the basement, and looked up at Arjun, wondering why he'd gone down there.

'Did you find anything interesting?'

'I'm still running through them,' he replied.

Tripathi entered the room and passed a list of names to Arjun.

'What's this?' Rajveer asked.

'A current list of every girl who has been reported missing in Varanasi.' Arjun flicked through the half dozen pages and with a red pen circled a dozen names.

'I've marked the Dalit girls in red,' he said, passing the list over to Rajveer.

'So you agree the killer's only targeting Dalit girls?'

'I do, but there's more to it. The girls are all around the same age, and none of them were married. I doubt that's a coincidence. Then the locations – the locations are getting closer to Varanasi, and the time between the murders is getting shorter.'

Arjun turned his attention to the map, which had pins showing the location of each murder. With his pen he drew a line linking each location, carrying it through to the centre, to the heart, of Varanasi.

'He's coming here?' Rajveer asked.

'No… he's already here,' Arjun replied. Standing beside her, he took the opportunity to ask her a direct question.

'If these girls were not Dalits, would more have been done? I mean, a handful of officers buried in a back office on the hunt for a serial killer? To be honest, I was expecting more.'

'You heard what Mehra said – he's doing what we can. Whether you believe that or not is up to you. I'm as new to this case as you are, and I can assure you of one thing: my team and I will do everything we can.'

'I'll hold you to that,' said Arjun as he took the pages from Rajveer's hand. Keeping hold of one page with three girls' names marked in red, he passed the others back to Rajveer to divide up among the team.

'I want face-to-face verification that they're safe – nothing less. If you can't find them, their names stay on the list.'

NINETEEN

Midday, Varanasi

The unit divided into three groups. Arjun headed out alone, while Rajveer split her officers into two teams, one led by her and the other by Tripathi. Arjun made his way to the old city, while Rajveer headed east, to the fringes of Varanasi. She turned the jeep off the highway, drove down an uneven lane, and entered a makeshift shantytown. She stopped outside a cluster of shacks. Under their wooden roofs there were food stalls, workshops and local merchants, making and selling everything you could think of.

The residents were largely labourers, Dalits among them. Rajveer asked around until she found the shack she was looking for. The vendor was a father of three, and his eldest daughter was on the list. He sold paans – betel leaves filled with tobacco and nuts. He rolled three as Rajveer stepped in, as her officers gathered a crowd of passers-by. Here, the locals greeted the police with humble offerings, for which no payment was made – more out of fear than kindness. Her officers took the paans without a second thought; Rajveer declined hers but offered to pay, but the vendor declined. She showed him the list: his daughter's name was at the top. She kept hold of the girl's photograph from the file.

'I'm looking after her case.'

'Madam, she's back,' said the father, but seemed reluctant to say any more. Rajveer insisted on seeing the girl. The father tried in vain to reassure her she was safe, but Rajveer insisted. Her officers came towards her as a crowd gathered.

'Then show me, now!' The crowds speculated about the purpose of the police's visit, much to the irritation of the girl's father. He turned his back on them and went behind the half-wall, and from there he brought his daughter into sight, still holding her back from the front stall. Her eyes were downcast but it was her: the girl from the photograph.

'Janki?' Rajveer asked. The girl nodded, still looking down. Her father sent her back and yelled at everyone to leave him alone. He said to Rajveer, coldly, 'I wish she was dead. She ran away with a city boy, and only returned when her fun was over. No one who knows this will marry her – she has cast a shadow on my remaining daughters.'

'Enough,' said Rajveer. 'She's still your daughter! If anything bad happens to her, I'll hold you responsible.'

She left, agitated by the man's words. He no longer felt any love for his daughter, but saw her as a burden. No wonder, when girls disappeared, even by no fault of their own, they'd choose never to return home, because their disappearance would always cast a shadow over their lives and their families. Rajveer had seen this all too often, and – like in this case – was powerless to do anything other than make an empty threat to the father.

TWENTY

Arjun arrived at Manikarnika Ghat; a sacred cremation ground surrounded by ancient temples, the ground stained by centuries of smoke and ash. Young and old, rich and poor – for the faithful, there was no greater place for their flesh to cease and their soul to be freed to attain eternal moksha – a liberation from the material world, to become one with the universe and God. Corpses were lined up, along with mourners, waiting their turn in sombre silence. The crackle and spit of burning pyres mingled with the chatter of a small army of funeral workers. Among them were priests, fire stokers and woodcutters.

Arjun arrived at the woodcutters' mound. Choking on the dust, he went up to the first axe man. He was dark and lean, with a polished complexion from the constant sweat of his labour.

'I'm looking for Bholadas,' Arjun said as he flashed his CBI badge.

The man held his axe by his side and looked at another man, a few years his senior. He was busy weighing a bundle of firewood ready to feed the flames of the funeral pyres. A baby goat ran through the wooden stacks, chased by a small boy, who was barefoot and playful. In the depths of misery and death, life continued. He was the son of a woodcutter, bred with the smell of sawdust and ash in the air. Like his father and grandfather, his life was bound to the burning ghats.

'Bholadas?' Arjun asked. The second man stopped weighing, seeing Arjun's official card, and greeted him with praying hands. He drew towards him as Arjun approached, hoping he'd brought positive news of his missing daughter.

'Yes sir, I'm Bholadas.'

'It was your daughter who was travelling to Allahabad?' Arjun showed him the girl's photograph. The man held it with affection. His voice tired and croaky, he said, 'Yes, sir – have you found her?' He was desperate for news.

'No, nothing so far... did she have a return ticket?' Arjun asked.

'Yes, sir. I bought it for her, but she never arrived at my sister's home in Allahabad.' Bholadas broke down and wept, pleading for help. 'Sir, I went to the police station – they promised to find her, but the police asked me for money. Sir, we are poor, and at their mercy. Please, sir, bring her back to me.' Bholadas clutched at Arjun's feet. Arjun helped him up and consoled him as the woodcutter's friends watched, their saws and axes silent for a short while.

TWENTY-ONE

Assi, Old City, Varanasi

On the other side of the old city, beyond the terraces of Assi where the brick mills lay abandoned, inside a frail building, on the top floor, smoke fused with the light and filled the corner of a small room with a dreamy haze. The room was filled with photographs of a young girl. Beside a rag on the floor was a black sports bag, a container of petrol, and fresh Tulsi hanging around the photo frames. This wasn't a home in any sense, but a hideout for the killer.

The young man seemed to be preparing a celebration: he started by placing a slice of chocolate cake, and a candle, in front of the photo frame. The girl held beneath the glass – his love, his life – was Savitri. She was a local girl Kasi had befriended. Soon she became his muse, and as time passed, she became everything to him.

A scattering of the sun's rays broke through the splintered window. Kasi strung his fingers through them. He lit a candle and picked up his guitar, tuned it, and played, with a gentle caress, 'Happy birthday'. Occasionally, his rhythm faltered as he remembered a broken promise: one he'd made to his beloved Savitri. He remembered the two of them enjoying the shade under a banyan tree, sitting back to back. He had been playful and in good spirits, thinking of a future far from Varanasi, the two of them travelling across the country. The photographer and his muse, on a motorbike ride from Shimla to Chennai and everywhere in between. She had dreams as well, but hers were less demanding: she was happy to be with him – nothing more, nothing less, just the two of them. He reassured her that her dream was his too.

'I'll speak to your brothers. I'll make them understand. After all, they only want what's best for you. I can give you everything they never could – what more could they want?' said Kasi.

'Promise me you'll never leave me. No matter what happens, you'll always be with me – promise me.' Savitri turned and buried her face in his chest. He felt the beating fear of her heart: she was afraid to lose him. Her brothers would never consent to their being together.

'I promise,' he said. 'In this life and the next, I promise, I'll always be yours as you are mine.'

Kasi again whispered the promise he had made to her in the shade of the banyan tree. As he did so, his fingers stalled and the guitar fell silent. Then the candle flame snuffed out. He found his tortured reflection in the photo frame and touched Savitri's face.

'I will free you, I promise you.'

TWENTY-TWO

The Mission

With less than an hour to lunchtime, the courtyard kitchen was busy with the sound of stoking stoves and the chopping of fresh onions. The menu was basic, with the usual bread, rice, dhal and a vegetable mash. But it was made with love, and no child ever went hungry. Helen finished filling a bucket with water and brought it over to the wooden table. The canopy hanging over the table provided much-needed shade from the midday sun. She soaked the potatoes in the bucket to soften their skins and wash the dirt off before peeling them. Agatha looked at her with pride. Helen had simply fitted in.

'The children you teach – how old are they?' Agatha asked.

'Oh, between five and seven, mainly. They're easy to manage at that age,' replied Helen.

'Sounds like you enjoy it.'

'I do. I'm not sure what else I would be good at. Seems that it runs in the family – Mum always said I took after you, especially when I told her I wanted to be a teacher.' Agatha stopped cutting her onions and looked at Helen. It was time to change the subject.

'Ram will be taking the food down to the children soon. Why don't you go with him? I told Maya you were here – she runs the mission school. When I told her you were a teacher, she insisted, in fact demanded, I introduced you. She's got her hands full as always and – well, she could do with the extra help. How about it?'

'I'd love to – it beats peeling potatoes,' said Helen, a smile on her face.

Agatha started chopping again, only to stop once more as Helen ventured into the past.

'Mum mentioned you were engaged once. Didn't you want a family of your own?" Agatha looked down, a tear brewing in her eye, and took a moment to think through her reply. It was the start of a conversation that would bring up a name she'd not uttered for many years.

'You mean David,' Agatha said. 'We were all set to get married, but… David was involved in a road accident. At first it looked like he'd pull through, but a few days later his heart stopped, and he was gone – and my dreams with him.'

'That's so sad,' said Helen.

'I tried my best to move on, but I found it too hard and…' Agatha trailed off and wondered whether this was the moment to tell Helen the truth – that she had been pregnant when David died.

'I was…' The words escaped her. 'I couldn't cope any more, and so I packed my bags and left and started a new journey in my life, halfway around the world.'

'Mum told me you were there at my birth, that you were the first person to hold me,' said Helen.

'Yes, I was – you were so delicate,' Agatha replied, dropping her guard.

TWENTY-THREE

An endless line of tiffin's, stacked tin lunchboxes passed through the sisters' hands, and they filled each one with a hot meal. As the lid was sealed on the final one, it was left to Ram to load them on either side of his old bicycle. The tiffins dangled from hooks screwed into several wooden staffs balanced over his cycle frame. There was no room to sit on the bike and ride it; he walked along, pushing the cycle. The tiffins clanged against one another as he made his way down the cobbled lane. Helen followed him. Ram spoke very little English and Helen spoke even less Hindi, so their conversation was largely an exchange of smiles and pointing as they headed in the direction of the mission school. It wasn't long before they had left the village behind and crossed into the open grasslands. Ahead of them was the hilly woodland beyond the Varuna River, which cut through the rising banks on either side. The river flowed into the Ganges a little way ahead. Apart from a handful of wooden shacks on the bank, there was a wooden footbridge straddling the Varuna, bringing life from one side to the other.

A steady stream of pedestrians crossed over, along with the occasional motorcycle, the husband steering in front, his wife holding him from behind. The narrow space between the ropes and uneven planks that paved the bridge made every crossing an adventure, but the locals crossed the bridge without a second thought. Helen watched, studying the locals crossing casually while another motorcycle pushed its way through, forcing the pedestrians to the sides – but even then, no one held on to the rope. She looked at Ram as he paid the bridge toll collector, then it was her turn. For a moment she expected Ram to follow the same path, but when he pointed to the bridge their direction became clear. The mission school lay on the other side, through the forest, and the only way to get there was over the bridge. Ram took the lead and, like the others, he simply went about his business, crossing each plank like an expert tightrope-walker who had walked the same rope a million times. Ram plucked at his teeth as he walked across.

The cycle and tiffins bobbled with each step; he seemed more concerned about dislodging a small bean stuck in between his teeth than the sway of the footbridge. He didn't look down once; he knew every plank and every gap.

Helen stepped onto the bridge, crossing the slats until she reached a gap. She held the ropes on either side, but was forced to let go of one side as she was preventing others from crossing. Ram didn't notice, and kept walking. Helen was nervous, afraid to take another step. Then, from behind, a small hand tugged at her shirt. It was a local boy, about seven years old, who had been sent by the toll collector to help Helen across. He offered his hand; she took it and followed his steps as she held on to the rope on one side. The river passed beneath them, only a few metres away, but it wasn't the drop that bothered Helen. It could have been one metre or a hundred metres; she just didn't like the sensation of the bridge wobbling. She felt silly to be led by a child, and close to the end she let his hand go and crossed over the final slats more confidently. The boy clapped as she crossed the final plank and stepped onto the bank. He was joined by Ram and others, clapping in amusement. The boy didn't wait to be thanked by Helen, and rushed back across the footbridge.

'Show-off,' shouted Helen as she waved him goodbye.

Ram guided her on, along the dry, well-trodden mud path through the forest and to a clearing close to the river. There she got her first sight of the mission school, an old stone building covered by a thatched roof and bamboo slats. She could hear children singing, and as she came closer the joy of each word lifted her spirits. Helen loved children, and hearing them singing cheered her up.

'If you're happy and you know it, clap your hands! If you're happy and you know it, clap your hands! If you're happy and you know it, and you really want to show it, if you're happy and you know, it clap your hands!' sang the children, joined by Maya and her assistant. Maya was small and dark-complexioned, with beautiful bold smoky eyes.

She was dressed in simple clothes. The mission school was her life. She often said that her life had started there when she was taken in as an orphan. Over the years, as others left, she stayed and finally took over the running of the school. It was more like a gang made up of thirty-something children of various ages all from the same caste, Dalits. They, like her, were orphans but, now with the help of the mission, they were forged into a family. Maya was assisted by Bella, the first to pick up on the familiar clanging of the tiffins approaching. She checked her watch; it was lunchtime. The children stopped singing as Ram appeared.

'OK, OK, I see lunch has arrived,' said Maya, noticing Helen besides him.

'I guess you must be Helen?'

'And you must be Maya – but please, don't stop on my account,' said Helen as the younger children swarmed around her.

'Don't worry; they do that to all our guests.'

'They're lovely, I've never felt so welcome.'

'OK, that's enough, everyone – shh… shh. Now, everyone, with big smiles and loud voices, I want you all to welcome our new friend, Ms Helen.'

'Welcome to our family, Ms Helen, welcome to our home. With lots of love and lots of kisses, we hope that in Varanasi you will fulfil your dreams and wishes,' said all the children with gusto, rushing at the end as Ram took the lids off the tiffins. They formed a line, with the youngest in front, as Ram passed out the tiffins.

'They're wonderful,' said Helen.

After lunch, the children were split up into groups, with a dozen or more sitting with Maya and Helen, and the rest with Bella, cooling their feet and being playful in the river. A herd of buffalos had joined them, enjoying the cool water in the heat of the sun.

'Life must be hard for them,' said Helen. It was evident the children had very little material goods, with their worn clothing and rundown school. But she didn't pity them:

in fact, she admired them. They seemed content with the cards that had been dealt to them.

'We try our best. They're everything I have: they're my family,' replied Maya. She turned her attention to a shy little boy sitting quietly next to her. His name was Raju. He'd latched on to Helen's shawl, which she held loosely on her lap. Helen made an attempt to befriend him, offering her open palm, fingers spread out for him to touch, but he just stared at her, his hands firmly at his side.

'He's not used to touching people,' said Maya. 'He's just a boy, but the stigma of his caste has had an effect on him.' Helen went to touch his nose, to break the ice, but Raju pulled away, taking her shawl with him, and ran off into the trees.

'Hey, Raju! Come back, Raju,' shouted Maya.

'It's OK, he's just playing. I'll get him back if that's OK?' said Helen. Maya agreed, and Helen headed into the trees.

TWENTY-FOUR

The forest closed in the further Helen ventured into it. The trees appeared older and their branches were heavy, blocking out the sunlight. Ahead of her, the path was deserted, with no sign of Raju. She stopped to listen for him moving. For a short while, there was nothing to hear but the sound of crows. She looked all around her and waited. A snap of a tree branch came from one side, and she went over to take a look. Behind the bushes was Raju. She'd already spotted him, looking back at her through the branches, but she played along for a while longer and, with her back turned, he took off once again. She ran after him into the bushes, calling out his name. Through a gap in the bushes, she found him.

But he was not alone. He was with a man. She found Raju's eyes glued to the man's. His hand rested on Raju's head, pinning him to the ground. The man held as still as a tree, unconcerned by Helen's presence. The forest was his home, and Helen was an uninvited guest.

The man had a scruffy look about him. He wore a worn, holey crimson shawl wrapped around his body. His hair was long and shaggy. He was unshaven, with long nails and bare feet. His skin, in parts, was covered by a patchy coating of dried mud. He carried all he owned in a pouch, and held a wooden staff. Middle-aged and thin, he carried no weight he didn't want. The locals called him by many names – to some he was a rogue, a vagabond, and to others a philosopher, a holy man. He was a stranger who kept little company and lived between the forest and riverbanks of the Varuna. He lived from day to day with a simple belief: to have nothing, is everything – and he had nothing.

For a man who had nothing, Nana seemed to have an unbreakable hold over Raju, and for a brief moment Helen found herself physically unable to move. She willed her hand forward but it wouldn't move. Nana noticed the pendant around her neck, and released Raju. Helen snapped back to her senses. Finding her will restored, she pulled

Raju back, keeping her eye on Nana. He didn't interfere, and said nothing. Apparently, he meant no harm to either of them. Helen backtracked with Raju through the bushes but, before they closed behind her, she couldn't help but turn and look back. Nana was gone.

TWENTY-FIVE

It was late afternoon under the searing sun when a familiar face arrived at the mission school. It was Arjun, bringing with him a bag of goodies: colouring books and pens as well as sweets. He greeted Maya as the children gathered around him, anxious to see what gifts he bore. He was an old friend. Helen returned with Raju.

'I was wondering where you were,' said Maya.

'We were just playing,' replied Helen. 'Hi,' she said, recognising Arjun from the night before.

'I see Agatha's keeping you busy.'

'Between the mission and here, I think I got a good deal. What brings you here?'

'Arjun's an old friend, but an absent one,' said Maya. Helen left them to it and joined Bella and the children.

'I know this will sound strange, but I don't think you should go anywhere alone for a while – just for a few weeks. You must know about the recent murders,' said Arjun.

'Is that why you're here?' Maya asked.

'I can't say much, it's an ongoing investigation, but there's a… Dalit connection, I'm sure of it.'

Maya stopped in her tracks.

'The killer is preying on young women, and I believe he's moving closer to the city. I can feel that things are going to come to a head soon.'

'I'll let Bella know. You'll take care, right? Why don't you stay for a while?'

'Another time. I just wanted to pass by and well… Maya, take care.' Arjun left.

As he disappeared, Maya returned to the children, Arjun's words still in her mind.

'Everything OK?' asked Helen.

'Sorry, yes, all fine,' replied Maya. 'You've settled in well, joined our family…' Maya noted the ease with which Helen had embraced the children, and they her. Helen felt secure among them: their innocence attracted her. They asked for nothing. Her own childhood came to her mind. For a moment she looked lost. Back in her childhood, she found herself cradling her best friend, Daisy, a rag doll, which she held tightly as she crouched in a corner of her old bedroom, shivering. Unlike these children, she had had two parents, but at times she had wished she was an orphan.

'Hey,' Maya tapped her, 'now you seem lost.'

'Oh, sorry. Must be the heat,' said Helen as she sat down. Maya brought some water over to her.

'By the way, I came across a strange man in the forest,' said Helen.

'Let me guess – mesmerising eyes, covered in dirt, looks like a beggar?'

Helen nodded.

'That must be Nana. Did he frighten you?'

'No – well, kind of.'

'He's harmless, really – a bit of a loner, comes and goes as he pleases. A well-spoken rogue of sorts. I didn't realise he was back.'

'He seemed to have a hold of Raju. When I found him, he was, well, in some kind of trance. I felt it too.'

Maya looked over at Raju and saw him playing with a group of boys. 'He seems just fine to me. Like I said, Nana's no trouble.'

A hundred metres away, behind the bushes, a pair of eyes peered through the foliage. The man's breathing was silent as he watched Helen from afar. It was Nana.

TWENTY-SIX

Night, the Mission

The hour was late, and the courtyard filled with moonlight. Under the arches, Agatha stoked the metal teapot, roasting over a coal fire. By the light of several lanterns, Helen waited for a cup of tea, book in hand. She'd picked it up earlier. It was filled with photos of the old city. She'd skipped to the chapter on the Aghori, the naked holy men of Varanasi, who were revered for their mystical powers. It was widely accepted that millions of middle-class city dwellers across India worshipped them, many in secret, unable to openly confess their devotion to them, fearing they would be seen as illogical in their desire to follow the Aghori's extreme ways.. The photo of one reminded her of the ghostly priest she had come across that night by the banks of the Ganges. His eyes leaped from the glossy page, and she recalled Nana's stare.

'Here.' Agatha poured the tea into a handmade red clay cup. It gave the tea a more earthy taste. 'Be careful, it's very hot.'

'Can I ask you something?' asked Helen.

Agatha looked up. 'Of course you can.'

'In all this time, you never came back to see us. Did something happen between you and Mum?'

'No, nothing of the sort. The truth is, I wanted to come back at first, then weeks turned into months, and years passed by. The familiar became less so, and Varanasi – well, it became home.'

'No regrets?' asked Helen.

Agatha said no, it was too late to make amends. So much had happened since she'd left, so much time had passed, but she had her own questions to ask. Sarah's death – her suicide – troubled her.

'I'd like to ask something about Sarah. Do you have any idea why she would take her own life? Did Jack have something to do with it?'

Helen turned away on hearing her father's name, but there was no escaping it. Agatha persisted until she answered.

'I never understood how the two of them got together. They were so different, but she stayed with him, even with all the lies, the drinking... and then the affairs, and...'

'And what? Go on,' Agatha encouraged her on, sensing she was holding back.

'She should have left him a long time ago.'

'Sarah was strong – nothing like me. She'd have done anything to keep the family together: that's who she was.'

Helen responded bitterly. 'And where did it get her? All these years, she was never happy. I know, I saw it in her eyes. She was tired and cold; he'd drained her. I'm sorry, Aunt Agatha, but you won't understand.'

'Then make me understand, Helen,' Agatha pleaded. She held Helen's hand but Helen was in no mood to open up. Instead she retreated, as she always did.

'It won't bring her back.' Helen put her tea down and stepped out into the open courtyard, where she looked up into the clear night sky. She tried to make out a few stars – anything to change the conversation.

'Helen.'

'It's been a long day. I'm going to bed. Goodnight, Aunt Agatha.' She left Agatha wanting – she had more questions to ask and it was evident Helen was hiding something; something to do with her father, perhaps.

Resting on her bed, Helen flicked through the pages of the book as a candle guttered by her side. Her finger stuck to the page, as she read the text under the photographs. One photo was of a man seated on a corpse as one would sit on a comfortable couch, with crossed legs, his eyes closed; the Aghori was praying. The photographs on the next page were equally menacing: one was of a half-open skull, filled with water, held in the grip of a true believer. The candle wick flickered in the breeze, it's little light scrabbling across the walls and onto the page. Helen's pulse raced a little faster. She turned the page and read on, the words and photographs compelling. She could have stopped, but the pages kept turning, drawing her in. She found herself among seers, healers and holy men – rogues to others, masters of spells and curses. They were famed for healing the soul, and hers was tortured. The next page caught her by surprise. It had one large image of an Aghori. Silver ash adorned his skin. His black eyes hit her. She lingered on them for far too long. She stiffened as she realised his eyes reminded her of Nana's.

Helen snapped the book shut. She'd seen enough to trouble her mind and ensure she had a restless night.

TWENTY-SEVEN

The morning had barely broken when a small tractor ground its way down a narrow track between two fields of sugarcane. The farmer steered, his young son lying in the trailer behind, feasting on bread as he was thrown around during the bumpy ride. The dog by his side snapped its teeth and licked its mouth with a hungry tongue, growling for some bread. The boy tore off a piece and fed him. The dirt below was tough and dry. As the tractor moved at a lazy pace, the boy leaped off with his dog and raced ahead and into the crops. The dog ran alongside him as the boy pushed his way through the crops. It wasn't long before he lost him.

'Bali?' the boy called, for that was his dog's name.

'Bali!' he shouted again, but he couldn't hear anything other than the chugging of his father's tractor. He moved ahead, pushing the crops back, and continued to call out. He drifted away from the track, and the sound of the tractor dulled as he found himself close to the wooden barn. He looked around and shouted once more: 'Bali!'

The dog responded with a torrent of barks – he was close. The boy headed towards the barks and found Bali scraping at the mud, sniffing the ground beneath the shade of a banyan tree. Something was troubling him.

The boy was puzzled by Bali's actions. The mud where he was sniffing looked different – it looked as though it had been turned from underneath. It was dark in colour and raised a little higher than the surrounding ground. The boy stepped to the dog's side and helped him pull the dirt away. Then the boy's fingers touched something that made him jump back. Bali stayed and licked what he'd unearthed, sniffed it then licked it again. The boy caught his breath as he saw a human nose pierce the dirt. He scrambled up and cried out for his father.

'Papa, Papa!' The boy tore through the crops, coming out on the track. He waved his father down, who stopped his tractor.

73

'What are you doing? What's wrong?' he asked. Clearly the boy was disturbed. He got out of the tractor and walked to his son and held him, trying to comfort him.

'What's wrong?' he asked again.

'I've found something, Papa.'

The boy pointed to the banyan trees next to the barn.

TWENTY-EIGHT

East of Assi, Maya arrived at the steps of Tulsi Ghat. She laid a flower on the temple mount and made her way down the steps until she arrived in front of the Ganges. A small crowd of dawn worshippers had gathered around a young priest as he rang in the arrival of the sun. Bells echoed from ghat to ghat down the river bank as the sun rose above the horizon. Across the river, there was an empty expanse filled only by white sand dunes and a forest. It seemed as if God had chosen the perfect spot from where to announce the morning.

The priest lit his candle, raised it towards the rising sun and recited the morning puja. Maya sang along as she did each morning, welcoming the day. Draped in a simple white saree, she dipped her feet in the Ganges and took her blessing from the river. And when she was done, she looked east and saw an elderly man. He'd become a familiar fixture in recent weeks. He was frail, starved of life and desperate to die. His thin frame sank into a wooden chair that was pulled on poles by two men from a nearby ashram. Robed in red and saffron cloth, he managed a brief smile when he saw Maya, who prayed for him with closed hands. He greeted her blessings with a blink. Barely breathing, he slouched to one side and watched across the river, waiting, praying that his life would end. He prayed each day for the same. His only wish was to return each morning until his will was done. His body was broken and dead – all that remained was his soul, and he was ready for it to be taken.

Further east along the ghats, Arjun was halfway through his morning run. He maintained a brisk pace as he made his way through the cobbled alleys of the old city. He passed by sights he remembered from childhood. Temples carved into the walls, doors that led to a labyrinth of alleys, and carvings cut into stones. The old city was alive with gods and mortals.

As Arjun strolled through an alley, a young man rolled out from inside a cavern gouged into a side wall. No bigger than a coffin and far less comfortable, it still provided him with shelter. Life crept in: dust was brushed away by the morning sweepers, a child sat beside a tea stall, fresh flowers were hung around idols. Fresh fruits and vegetables appeared on the mats, freshly rolled roti cooked in sizzling frying pans, a spoonful of peas and gravy by its side as a line of customers formed, some still brushing their teeth with freshly stripped neem twigs as they waited their turn.

Arjun sweated out his thoughts, running through the jigsaw of the case, piecing together key facts, murder by murder. His thoughts were disturbed by a sudden burst of noise: a priest's voice coming from a high-rise loudspeaker, one of many perched on lamp-posts across the old city. He ran out into the open air and rested on a terrace overlooking the Ganges. As he caught his breath, he watched the longboats sail past, full of tourists snatching glimpses of bathers in the water. A blanket of white cloths covered the steps as the washers dried their sheets. The priest's chants still echoed from the speakers, more pronounced in the absence of any walls to cushion his voice. Arjun walked across to the plateau and arrived at Assi. The place was marked by an old banyan tree, and favoured by foreign tourists. Arjun called over the tea boy and placed his order, adding an unhealthy slice of buttered toast to his request. Tea and toast on the riverbank. It wasn't New Delhi; it was home. As he waited for the tea to arrive, he noticed a police jeep pull up in between two tourist coaches. His phone rang at the same time: it was Rajveer. She was on her way to investigate the body that had been reported by the farmer. She'd sent Tripathi to collect Arjun. Arjun made his way over to the police jeep with the tea boy chasing behind him, but he was too late; his customer had gone.

TWENTY-NINE

Late Morning, The Farm

The farm land emptied as the labourers gathered around a cluster of police jeeps and an ambulance. A few – the more agile and curious – managed to climb a tree and get a bird's-eye view of the crime scene. A dozen officers held them back, occasionally having to use their police sticks to beat back the crowd. As the farmers and villagers speculated among themselves, more police officers cut through the sugarcane field, trampling down the crops as they created a multitude of new paths through the field, all away from the shrouded corpse still buried in the dirt.

Rajveer pulled out a pack of gum and offered it to the farm boy. He was a little reserved, so she put the whole pack in his hand and thanked him for answering all her questions.

'Madam, they're ready,' said an officer. Rajveer watched her officers, aided by two villagers, lift the girl's body out of the dirt and rest it on the ground. One of the farmers, choked by the stench of rotting flesh, rushed away, spewing his breakfast out in his hands. Rajveer covered her mouth with a cloth and knelt down. She observed the corpse carefully. The girl's face was bruised and swollen, her hands decayed and skin her blistered. Worms had been busy feasting on her innards. Rajveer examined the body from head to toe and then, with a firm hold, rolled it forward, enough to see the girl's back, where she found the knife wound. Gently she rolled her back.

She found the girl's side pocket and felt inside it. As well as some money, she found a folded bus ticket. Another jeep pulled up, and Arjun stepped out.

'What are you doing?' he asked angrily. 'Get those people back!' he ordered the officers, worried they would overrun the crime scene and contaminate the evidence. Not that any care had been taken by Rajveer and the other officers. They'd already made a mess. In every direction, the ground was covered with officers' footprints. Any of the footprints could have belonged to the killer, but the officers' prints had killed off any chance of him applying his normal forensic tests. He knelt by Rajveer's side and didn't hold back from venting his disdain of her lack of control.

'You can't do this – you're leaving your fingerprints all over the evidence! And the officers, look, they're just walking over everything.'

'Look, this is how we work here. If you want to try something different, be my guest.'

'What's the point? They've messed this one up.'

'In that case, take a look at this.' She passed him the ticket, held between her finger and thumb. He took it from her carefully by one corner, taking care not to add his fingerprint to hers.

'I found it inside her pocket: a return ticket from Allahabad to Varanasi.'

Arjun remembered the woodcutter: his daughter had gone missing on her way to Allahabad.

'I think I know who she is. I visited a woodcutter yesterday. His daughter was reported missing and on our list. She had taken the bus to Allahabad but never arrived. Who found her?' he asked.

'The farmer's son,' Rajveer replied, pointing to the father and son squatting under a nearby tree.

'I've already spoken to them. They didn't see anyone.'

Arjun noticed Bali playing with the boy. He went over to see him.

'What's his name?' he asked the boy.

'Bali,' he replied.

'That's a nice name. And what's your name?'

'Sham.'

'It's nice to meet you, Sham. I know you've been helping that lady over there' – he pointed to Rajveer – 'but I'd like to ask you for help as well. Is that OK?'

The boy nodded in agreement.

'I'd like to borrow Bali for a few minutes. Is that OK with you?'

The boy passed Arjun the string tied around Bali's neck: 'as long as you bring him back.'

'Promise.' Arjun befriended Bali, letting him sniff his hand and take his scent. Arjun headed back to the corpse, tugging Bali behind him. He asked the officers and Rajveer to stand back and allow Bali to sniff the girl's clothes. He helped him along by tearing a small piece from her top and letting Bali sniff at it. Bali barked and tugged Arjun in the direction of the barn. Arjun broke his string and let him loose, and he ran straight to the barn, and waited below the window through which the girl had escaped. Bali sniffed the mud prints and found a trail through the crops. Arjun followed closely behind him. Bali raced ahead, sniffing all the way, sometimes changing direction, only to return to the path the girl had taken. They arrived at the bent and crushed stalks, half as high as the others. Beyond them was the dirt track. Bali sniffed at the dirt and walked ahead, but the scent was gone. Arjun deduced this was as far as the girl had got.

Arjun crouched down in the dirt and in the dry earth found the gouges and scars left by the girl's fingers as she had tried in vain to claw her way out. He stepped up and wiped the dust off himself as he looked down the dirt track and saw a motorbike on the horizon. He watched it as it sped past, and wondered whether anyone could have seen the girl.

Soon afterwards, he returned to the corpse. Rajveer had finished taking photographs, but before the body was loaded onto a stretcher, Arjun took a final close-up look. He noticed the dirt under her nails; he was right about the gouges. He moved up to her neck and then her face, and stopped. There was something wedged between her teeth, barely visible and easily missed. He looked for a tool to pick it out, but he had nothing to hand. Then he turned to Rajveer and without warning he plucked a hair clip from her head. Rajveer snapped, 'Excuse me.'

But he was too busy to be polite and ask. He carefully pulled down the lower jaw, which was still tight. He pushed a little harder to unhinge the teeth, which were clenched. He got the jaw open just enough to insert the clip inside and with a surgeon's hand he pinched the object inside and pulled it out slowly. Holding it in the clip, he took a closer look. It was dark green; some sort of mushed leaf. He wasn't sure, so he sniffed at it. He recognised the plant's scent over the smell of the rotting corpse.

'Tulsi,' said Arjun without hesitation. He had every reason to be confident, as the scent of Tulsi was engraved on his memory. He recalled the day his mother died: the priest had brought with him a fresh bushel of Tulsi leaves and selected from them the most pungent, and placed them inside his mother's mouth. It was the last thing he remembered before his mother's corpse was cremated. He later asked his father why the priest had placed the Tulsi in his mother's mouth, and his father had explained that Tulsi was used because its strong scent would attract the attention of the gods, so when the fires consumed his mother's flesh her soul would be freed and taken by the gods.

'Did you find any Tulsi at any of the other sites?' he asked Rajveer.

'No, I don't recall we did. Besides, it wouldn't have survived, as those bodies were burned. Where are you going with this?'

'I'm not sure, but one thing is clear – the girl made a run for it. She broke out of the barn and ran through the fields to reach the road – and that's as far as she got. But he didn't burn her, and in a final act he's chosen to place Tulsi in her mouth. Why would you kill someone and then follow the last rites and place Tulsi in their mouth?'

Neither of them had any answers, but Rajveer knew a man who could shed some light on the matter. He was a professor who lectured at the city's Sanskrit College, and who'd spent most of his life living in the past. He was sharp, witty and could recite any line or verse anyone requested from ancient epic poems. Arjun agreed to visit him. He had a request to make of Rajveer.

'Once the girl's identity is confirmed, I'd like to break the news to her father, if that's OK.'

'Sure.' Rajveer agreed.

THIRTY

Afternoon, Varanasi Markets

The market was alive with stalls doing a brisk trade as crowds of pilgrims exchanged their hard-earned cash for spiritual trophies. Their desire to free themselves from material things was briefly abandoned as they filled their bags with idols, books and copper-sealed Ganges pots – anything and everything they could get their hands on to show their family and neighbours back home they had captured the magic of Varanasi. But not everything was moving; the traffic around the market had ground to a halt. Lines of rickshaws and free-roaming buffalo fought among themselves for every inch of space, as the traffic cop blasted his whistle, unable to move the tide along. The problem was caused by the arrival of a famous sadhu – a spiritual leader adored by his followers, who showed up in their hundreds to follow him through the old market and on to the ghats to bathe with him in the Ganges.

'What's the problem?' asked Maya, inside the back of a rickshaw with Helen.

'The usual pilgrims – they've taken over the place. No one cares about their safety; they just walk wherever they want,' said the frustrated driver as he blasted his horn. It wasn't a good move, as others copied, and within seconds a chorus of rickshaw horns serenaded the pilgrims, who chanted and beat their drums with a competitive zeal.

Maya decided it was time to make the rest of their journey on foot. She settled up with the driver, who demanded extra for the time he'd spent waiting in the traffic, but she paid what she felt was fair and left.

Maya grabbed Helen as a motorbike rider threaded his way through any gap he could find. Inch by inch, he horned his way forward, yelling at pilgrims to get out of his way. Tied to the back of his bike, on a rack, was a corpse wrapped in ritual cloth. It was laid horizontally across the rack: the rider had travelled from Mirzapur, some sixty kilometres south-west of the city, to fulfil the wishes of the deceased to be cremated on the ghats of the Ganges. Another corpse appeared behind him, stacked on top of a rickshaw and tied to its roof like a bundle of luggage. Inside the family sat quietly, dazed by the traffic.

The area around the market was flooded with corpses: everywhere Helen looked, she found them – tied on the back of motorbikes, on trucks, on rickshaw tops, and held above their heads by mourners who were carrying them.

'Let's get out of here.' Maya and Helen submerged themselves in Varanasi. The alleyways ran for kilometres, meandering and spreading through the old city like a tree's roots clawing out in search of water. Each one turned and twisted, lined with stalls selling anything from fresh fruit and pastries to idols and holy books. The two of them weaved their way through the crowds that funnelled past in both directions: some were mourners, others residents and others foreigners. Among them was a tourist circling the same spot, clearly lost.

Helen squeezed past a stubborn buffalo who'd decided to block the footpath. She watched passers-by taking blessings from it. It seemed everything – the temples, the worn stones around them, and the buffalo – was sacred. She felt like an intruder.

The chaos passed as they came close to the river bank. Emerging through a passage and down a steep set of stairs they arrived at the ghats, where the crowds were thinner and the river provided a breezy respite from the bustle of the town. Maya shouted out to a nearby stallholder, whose table was stacked high with mounds of fresh mangos.

'Oh my God,' she said. Maya hurried over to the stall. Like a child unable to choose from an array of toys, she looked for the ripe ones, touching their flesh and smelling them, much to the annoyance of the trader, who tried to hurry her up.

'You're mad,' Helen said, 'bloody mad.' She found Maya's burst of excitement hilarious.

'You won't understand; it's an Indian thing,' said Maya as she picked two ripe mangos from the stack. She'd handed over more cash than she had to, and forgot to collect her change.

Maya bit the tops off each mango and passed one to Helen. The other, she held above her mouth. Her head tilted, she squeezed the flesh, and from the cut the mango's juices flowed out, much to Maya's delight.

'Come on! What are you waiting for?' She helped Helen eat her mango the Indian way.

'Open, tilt your head back and big squeeze,' said Maya, as she positioned Helen for delivery.

Helen's lacked Maya's steady head. The juices flowed out over her face, only occasionally going into her mouth. The juice and pulp ran down her cheeks and neck.

Since her mother's death, this had been the first time Helen had felt so free, had been able to laugh so loudly, without hesitation. In Maya she'd found a free spirit to lose herself with – for a day, at least.

THIRTY-ONE

A saffron-robed priest threw grains of rice into the holy fire as it flickered under the protection of the temple dome. A beautiful young bride with her hands covered in henna and dressed in a shimmering red wedding dress followed her groom around the flames. Bound to one another by a holy thread, the bride took care to follow the groom's footsteps, as onlookers tossed fresh petals over their heads. Helen and Maya watched from one side as the bride and groom walked around the fire seven times. The priest recited the sacred seven vows, each of which were repeated by the bride and groom, the groom first.

The first vow was: 'O you who feeds life-sustaining food, nourish my visitors, friends, parents and offspring with food and drinks. O beautiful lady, I, as a form of Vishnu, take this first step with you for food.

Yes, whatever food you earn with hard work, I will safeguard it, prepare it to nourish you. I promise to respect your wishes, and nourish your friends and family as well.'

The second vow (for the groom) was: 'O,thoughtful and beautiful lady, with a well-managed home, with purity of behaviour and thought, you will enable us to be strong, energetic and happy. O beautiful lady, I, as Vishnu, take this second step with you for strength of body, character and being.

And the bride replied: 'Yes, I will manage the home according to my ability and reason. Together, I promise to keep a home that is healthy, strength and energy-giving.'

The third vow was: 'O, skilful and beautiful lady, I promise to devote myself to earning a livelihood by fair means, to discuss, and let you manage and preserve our wealth. O dear lady, I, as Vishnu, cover this third step with you to thus prosper in our wealth.'

The bride responded: 'Yes, I join you in managing our income and expenses. I promise to seek your consent, as I manage our wealth, fairly earned, so it grows and sustains our family.'

The fourth vow was: 'O, dear lady, I promise to trust your decisions about the household and your choices; I promise to dedicate myself to help our community prosper, and matters outside the house. This shall bring us respect. O my lady, I, as Vishnu, take this fourth step with you to participate in our world.'

The bride replied: 'Yes, I promise to strive to make the best home for us, anticipate and provide necessary things for your worldly life, and for the happiness of our family.'

The fifth vow was: 'O, lady of skill and pure thoughts, I promise to consult with you and engage you in the keeping of our cows, our agriculture and our source of income; I promise to contribute to our country. It shall win us our future. O my skilled lady, I, as Vishnu, take this fifth step with you to together grow our farms and cattle.'

The bride replied: 'Yes, I promise to help you and protect the cattle, our agriculture and business. They are a source of yoghurt, milk, ghee and income, all useful for our family, and necessary for our happiness.'

The sixth vow was: 'O, lovely lady, I seek you and only you, to love, to have children, to raise a family, to experience all the seasons of life. O my lovely lady, I, as Vishnu, take this sixth step with you to experience every season of life.'

The bride replied: 'Feeling one with you, with your consent, I will be the means of your enjoyment of all the senses. Through life's seasons, I will cherish you in my heart. I will worship you and seek to complete you.'

The seventh and final vow was: 'O friends! Allow us to cover the seventh step together: this promise, our Saptapad friendship. Please be my constant wife.'

And the bride replied: 'Yes, today, I gained you. I secured the highest kind of friendship with you. I will remember the vows we just took and adore you forever, sincerely, with all my heart.'

After the final vows, the priest pronounced them man and wife.

'Why do they walk around the fire like that?' Helen asked.

'It's a ritual that every bride and groom must follow – with the completion of each circle and vow, the two of them are bound together for eternity. So beautiful.'

'It is, but I'm not sure I'd want to be bound to the same guy for all eternity, though.'

'I believe, when you fall in love, it will be with one you loved many lifetimes before,' said Maya.

'It's a wonderful dream, but life's not so simple, is it? Things never pan out the way you think,' Helen replied. Her attention was caught by the sound of chanting close by, which grew louder.

'*Ram name Satya hey, Ram name Satya hey*' (Only truth is the name of Lord Ram), the mourners cried. The men passed less than a foot from her. The man's corpse was covered, but his face was exposed. He brushed close to her, and she gasped as he passed within an inch of her.

'I must seem strange seeing all this,' said Maya.

'Well, it's the first time I've seen a wedding and a funeral side by side,' replied Helen. The charm of the wedding had been forgotten as she dwelled on the corpse.

'I've had an idea. I need you to close your eyes,' said Maya.

'Why?' Helen asked.

'Just close them and trust me. Don't open them until I say so – promise me.'

Helen agreed, and Maya took her hands and guided her slowly through the intense chants and ringing of bells as they passed another temple. Helen could hear dogs barking, a monkey's cry, the crackles of fires, and in the breeze the engines of passing motor boats. She found herself stepping down a few times. The sound of children splashing in the river and the faint whispers of bathers' prayers greeted her as Maya sat her down. Helen felt calmed as the sounds blended into one another and in the absence of sight she absorbed everything the ghats had to offer.

'Open your eyes, Helen.'

She found herself on the steps overlooking the shimmering flow of the Ganges. The vista was so wide it filled her expanse. Maya said nothing to disturb her.

'My mother would have loved it here, I think.' Helen paused. 'She passed away a few weeks ago. That's why I'm here.'

'I'm sorry to hear that,' Maya consoled her.

Under the cover of a large umbrella, its fabric torn through age, Kasi, a tourist snapper turned his lens, framing Helen and Maya in his sights. Their blurred faces became clear as Kasi zoomed in. His pulse slowed, his breathing paused: his finger steady over the button, he waited for the moment to arrive. He found it when Helen's skin slightly fractured with affection, cutting a brief smile across her cheek. He pressed the shutter, and took a dozen shots, framed in a single pulse.

'How about you? Do you have any family?' Helen asked.

'Besides the children? Yes, I have a sister, her name's Chaya. She's a few years younger than me. I managed to get her into a good school with the money I've saved, and that's where she stays. I want her to have a good life.'

'Do you see her often?'

'Not much, but whatever time we get, we make the most of it. I'm seeing her later today, and we'll sing and dance and through the weekend.'

Maya was proud of her younger sister, and sent her what money she saved from her pay at the mission. She wanted everything for her, hoping she would live out her dreams.

Just then Helen spotted Maya's bracelet. It was wrapped around her wrist, a thickly engraved copper piece, with her name punched through it. 'That's beautiful,' remarked Helen.

'Chaya made it for me. She loves making things – she's an artist.'

Maya caught sight of an approaching photographer, his camera extended. He was clicking away with the energy of a fashion shoot, taking a mix of high and low shots and thrusting the camera close to them. His name was Sanjay; he was another tourist snapper: a stick-thin man, wearing a rip-off Ralph Lauren T-shirt with the label misspelled – not that he cared. His unlaced sport shoes were partially covered by overlong jeans. He wore a thick-framed pair of sunglasses, the kind usually worn by Italian film directors. Beaming with confidence, he sat without invitation next to Helen, and passed her his camera, with the viewer set to Play.

'Hi, I'm Sanjay... and what's your name?' He went straight for his sales pitch.

'Hey, what are you doing?' Maya asked.

'It's cool; I'm just catching the perfect shots of you lovely ladies. Don't believe me? Take a look.' Sanjay clicked through the photographs on the camera screen.

At first glance the stills were impressive: quick shots framed to indulge a tourist's ego. A closer inspection would have shown them for what they were: average.

Sanjay wasted no time in pitching his price to Helen: 1000 rupees to start with, an optimistic price, but he was soon ready to half it. However, Helen wasn't buying. Maya pushed his camera aside and confronted him. 'You should ask first. Come on, Helen, let's go.'

As they were about to move, Kasi interrupted them, nudging Sanjay to one side.

'Oy! What the hell. I was here first,' Sanjay tried to barge back in, realising his sale was falling through, but Kasi held firm.

'Let the lady decide,' said Kasi as he placed his camera in Helen's hand. 'If you don't like what you see, smash the camera. You decide.'

Kasi was patient: he didn't feel the need to flick through his shots as Sanjay did. For him, each still was as good as a painting.

He was good at reading faces, and seeing Helen's fixation on the frame, he knew he'd hooked her.

'It's good... very good, but I'm sorry, I'm not buying.' Helen passed the camera back to Kasi.

'And I'm not selling, just sharing – nothing more,' Kasi replied as Helen stood up. 'You arrived today? I've not seen you around before,' Kasi ventured.

Helen didn't reply.

'I'll see you around,' Kasi said.

He watched them leave, then turned his attention to the still in the viewfinder, ignoring Sanjay's curses, which only stopped when he found a new set of customers to pounce on: a boatful, newly arrived.

'Are you coming? There's enough work for both of us. We could work as a team. Hey... are you listening? What the hell's wrong with you?' Giving up, Sanjay left Kasi to himself.

Sanjay held out his hand to help the first tourist off the boat.

THIRTY-TWO

A string of palm-readers caught Helen's attention as Maya was examining a jewellery stall. She was looking for a gift for Chaya. The stallholder plucked out an old ring set with a well-polished, but cheap, gemstone and showed it to her. She liked its rich green colour.

'What do you think of this?' she asked Helen. 'Helen…?' She looked around and found Helen waving her over. She had gone down to the terrace and was waiting in front of a palm-reader as he finished with his current customer.

'Shit,' said Maya, who didn't like palm-readers.

'Come, come,' the palm-reader said to Helen. With his legs folded, he sat with a loincloth wrapped around him under the shade of a thatched umbrella.

'Helen, wait, Helen,' shouted Maya, trying to stop her from being fleeced by the man's false promises.

'It's just a bit of fun.' Helen pulled her down to join her.

'It's a waste of time,' said Maya.

'Give me your hand, come on,' Helen insisted.

The palm-reader watched as Maya sat in front of him, and his attitude changed. He refused to take Maya's hand, keeping his hands firmly by his side. He did, however, greet Maya with a nasty stare; she wasn't welcome. He jerked his head to brush her away. She could see his anger in his glare: how dare she sit in front of him?

'I told you it was a waste of bloody time.' Maya got up and gave the man a defiant snare. Helen, confused by his refusal, followed Maya.

'I'm sorry – why did he do that?'

'Same reason Raju was afraid to touch your hand. I'm a Dalit, like Raju – an untouchable. He believes I'm polluted; they all do. This place will never change until *they* do, and I'll be grey and old before that happens.'

As they moved away Helen turned around and found the palm-reader still staring after them, but his anger had faded. There was sorrow in his eyes.

'It's been a long day,' said Helen.

'It's been fun,' Maya replied. She checked her watch to make sure she had enough time to catch her bus, then Sanjay reappeared.

'Not you again! Get lost – we're not interested,' she said, but Sanjay kept after them as they moved out of the ghats and into the alleys. This time he was prepared, with prints in hand. He ran through them as he walked by Helen's side. As the path narrowed, Helen pulled out a few hundred rupees. It was the same amount she'd spend on a coffee back in London, and was enough to get rid of Sanjay before Maya punched him.

She slammed the money in his hand. 'Take it or leave it.' Sanjay wanted more – like any salesman, he'd caught his fish and now he wanted to reel her in, but on seeing a pair of police officers patrolling ahead, he took her offer and gave her the photographs.

'Enjoy them, Miss' he said as he counted his money.

The falling sun cast its shadow over the old city. As evening approached, the human traffic flowed in one direction. Away from the ghats, the masses spilled out into the markets and nearby bus stand. Maya was anxious to catch her bus, as the next one wasn't for two hours. As they emerged onto the square, Maya saw her bus. Blocking her path was a sea of people, and the bus was filling quickly.

'Sorry, I have to go,' she said as she shoved her way through the masses.

'Go, before you miss it. I'll see you soon.'

'Rickshaw…' Helen waved one down. She had an easier time as three were waiting in the square.

THIRTY-THREE

Sanskrit College

The dusky sky provided a perfect contrast to the splendour and majesty of the sandstone face of the Sanskrit College. As the police jeep swept in, the gothic building dominated the vista. If it hadn't been for the students dressed in their traditional nehru shirts and dhotis bottoms, instead of jeans, one could be forgiven for thinking they had arrived at the Palace of Westminster in London. Arjun stepped out of the jeep, and Rajveer asked for Professor Sharma's whereabouts. A student pointed to the side gardens, where the professor was lecturing a handful of his best and brightest students under the gaze of the swallows dancing between the trees.

Sharma was everything one would expect from a professor: grey-haired, conservative, witty and deceptively humble, and beneath his pristine shawl and poised exterior was a master of Vedic knowledge.

The professor was leaning back in his chair, a soft cushion to one side, and with his eyes closed he recited from memory the words shared between the great battle warrior Arjun and his friend and Lord, Krishna: words set in poems between a mortal and immortal during the battle of the Mahabharata. The professor always closed his eyes when he read from memory: he somehow found colour in his thought and brushed his words with a painter's touch, bringing each string of words to life in his thick Banarasi dialect. It added a bite to his recital. His narrative was interrupted on occasion as he stopped to relish the juices from the red tobacco paan that he chewed. A pot by his side was filled with his spit. He was everything any Indian expected a Banarasi to be, and he was proud of living up to the stereotype.

A wary porter reluctantly tapped the professor on the shoulder; he didn't take kindly to interruptions not of his own making. Breaking off from his tale, the professor glanced at the faces of his students and noticed they were all looking away from him, to their right. The sight of a police officer within college grounds was unusual.

"I admit it,' boomed the professor as he extended his hands, 'I'm ready to be cuffed. I killed him with my bare hands.' His words left his students in silence, their mouths hanging open. He was joking, of course. The warm embrace he gave Rajveer put an end to his humour, and left his students embarrassed. Some even believed his confession, as he'd expressed it with the same passion as his epic tales.

'Students – they believe anything you tell them,' he joked. He clapped his hands and ended the class.

'What brings you to my humble abode?' he asked Rajveer.

'I'm in need of your help,' Rajveer replied.

'My help? Well, that's a first. Please join me inside.' The professor led them under the arched veranda and into his office. As the light faded outside, the porter lit the oil lanterns. A flock of sparrows flew inside through an opening in the roof. They rustled around the scaffolds that held up the roof. The vast inner chamber was largely empty and in darkness, with just the shadow of the building's former glory.

As the professor went to his chair, he asked of Arjun, 'And who might you be?'

'Arjun Das, CBI.'

'CBI, from Delhi? You're far from home.'

'Not really; I was born in Banaras,' Arjun replied.

'Really? Which part?'

'Oh... Assi. I grew up there. My father was well known by the locals. His name was Krishna Das.'

The professor recalled the name. The city had expanded over the years, but the old district along the riverbank from Assi to Raj Ghat remained much the same, stuck in a time warp. In his younger days, the professor had often passed his Sunday afternoons at

Assi debating the ancient tales and scriptures with colleagues. Arjun's father had been well known in Assi around the same time. He regularly spoke up for the rights of his co-workers.

'You know, it's quite stuffy in here. Let's talk outside where it's cooler,' said the professor. His mood changed suddenly when he found out about Arjun's caste. The professor was a Brahmin, born into a priestly caste, the most conservative of all Hindus. Like his father before him, he followed the old ways that cemented the differences between castes. There was no room for moderation. He was not modern India, but a man who strongly believed in God – his god, who had created the priests to sit at the head of the body while the Dalit was left to serve at the feet. Arjun didn't miss the tell-tale signs; the sudden change in the professor's voice was all too familiar to him. Rajveer was ready to go outside, as the professor had suggested, but Arjun had other ideas.

'I agree, it is a bit stuffy in here,' said Arjun as he flipped the cover off the water pot and poured a full glass of water for himself. He drank it, then refilled his glass, along with a second one, as the professor looked on, silently fuming.

'Here, this should cool you down.' Arjun offered Rajveer a glass of water and left the second on the table for the professor as he sat down on the chair opposite the professor's empty one. Deliberately, he made himself comfortable, like an unwelcome guest who is finding enjoyment in knowing he is not welcome.

The professor found himself forced to come back in, and took his chair. He was greeted by Arjun's official CBI badge, which he placed firmly on the table to make sure the professor understood his authority.

'How can I help?' asked the professor, deliberately directing his words at Rajveer.

Rajveer kept to the morning's murder only, as the murder of the other four girls had not been officially linked to it, and the information had so far been kept out of the public domain.

'Can you shed some light on this?' she asked, as she told him about the Tulsi inside the girl's mouth. The professor turned his back on them and reached out to a stack of books on a shelf behind him, where several dozen were stacked in an uneven pile. He glanced down the books' spines, muttering the occasional title until he found the one he was looking for.

'Hmm… Tulsi, Tulsi,' he muttered again, flicking through the pages. 'A-ha!' he said when he found the page he wanted, and placed the open book in front of Rajveer.

'Tulsi,' he said, tapping the illustration of the plant, 'in ancient times it had a different form – that of a woman.'

'A woman?' asked Rajveer.

'Yes, a woman named Vrinda. It is said she was the greatest devotee of Lord Vishnu. Legend has it that she was married to a powerful war lord called Jalandhar, and because of Vrinda's devotion to Lord Vishnu, Jalandhar was blessed with the god's protection. This meant that no mortal or immortal – not even another god – could kill him.'

As the professor turned to the next illustration, Arjun and Rajveer began to make notes.

'Jalandhar, empowered by this protection, went on to slaughter all his enemies without mercy. God-fearing kings and farmers alike prayed to Lord Shiva for help, but Lord Shiva could do nothing. Can you imagine – the mighty Lord Shiva was helpless!' said the professor with a gesture of humour and disbelief. 'Lord Shiva turned to Lord Vishnu and told him, one god to another, that no mortal should have the power to defy the gods, and since he had created this problem it was up to him to fix it.'

Feeling the professor was getting side-tracked, Rajveer interjected.

'Professor, sir, I don't see how this helps our case.'

The professor raised his hand to halt her interruption. 'Wait, young lady, wait. What you are seeking may lie in the past.' The professor turned to the next page, where there was an illustration of a great battle.

'As Jalandhar was kept busy fighting another battle far away from his home, Lord Vishnu came to Vrinda in Jalandhar's form at night and violated her chastity. Deeply hurt by this betrayal, Vrinda broke her devotion to Lord Vishnu. As a result, Jalandhar lost his protection and Lord Shiva took the opportunity and killed him.' The professor slammed his hand down onto the table. 'Gone, Jalandhar gone!'

Rajveer and Arjun were drawn into the tale as the professor turned page after page.

'Deeply betrayed by Lord Vishnu, Vrinda cursed him, and in a final act she sacrificed herself on Jalandhar's burning funeral pyre.'

Arjun looked at Rajveer at the mention of the fire sacrifice. Rajveer circled the words *SACRIFICE* and *FIRE* on her notepad.

'Now, Lord Vishnu realised he had wronged Vrinda, so in an act of penance he immersed her soul into a seed that blossomed into Tulsi. Lord Vishnu also promised her soul that in his next incarnation he would marry her. Today we mark this bond every year with Tulsi Vivah, Tulsi's wedding to Lord Vishnu.'

'And what about the last rites? Do they always use Tulsi?' Rajveer asked.

'Yes, always. Tulsi is placed in the deceased's mouth and sometimes a Tulsi chain is placed around the neck; especially of a deceased woman. The Tulsi's strong scent is said to allow the gods to recognise the soul as it frees itself from the burning body.'

The professor sat back in his chair, his throat dry from all his talking. He reached out for the water glass, but stopped short of taking it. He glanced at his watch; he was done telling tales.

'Thank you, professor, you've been most helpful.' Rajveer got up.

'I hope I was some help. Please do stop by anytime, Rajveer,' he told her without extending the same invitation to Arjun.

Before they left Arjun had the last word. 'I'll certainly be in touch. Thank you, professor.'

The professor waited until he was sure they had gone, and then yelled out for the porter's attention. He came running, expecting to find the professor in trouble, but he wasn't in any physical danger. It was a spiritual danger: the professor had an urgent desire to be cleansed.

'Bring me a bucket of water,' he demanded as he shed his clothes. 'And bring me some clothes – anything you can find. Hurry.'

The professor cursed, angry that Arjun had dared to enter his space and drink from his glass. He felt invaded and polluted, and went round his room, throwing out the glasses, the water pot, his clothes and the chair Arjun had sat on – everything he could remember the polluter had touched. Everything else he thought he'd touched – a pen, a book – found themselves on the grass outside. The porter came back with fresh clothes, a shawl and a cloth to cover the professor's modesty.

'Clean it, all of it – wash the floor, the desk, everything,' the professor said, as he wrapped the cloth around his waist and covered himself with the shawl. He walked out to go home.

'Sir, what about all this?' The porter pointed to the things thrown out by the professor.

'Burn it, throw it away, I don't care. I just don't want it back in my office,' the professor replied as he walked away.

THIRTY-FOUR

Rajveer drove the jeep along the highway that led over the main iron bridge, heading back to the police station. Unbeknown to her, a few hundred metres away, under the iron bridge, the fifth girl, gagged and tied, fought Kasi. Above her a train rolled over the bridge, shaking its foundations, draping her with a veil of dust. Her eyes squinted as specks of dust fell in her eyes. Her black mascara – a tradition among Hindu women to fend off evil – failed to protect her. She wore a fresh garland of Tulsi and had been doused in petrol: all Kasi had left to do was light her up.

Two fishermen, resting for the night on board their boat, which was moored upstream at the mouth of the Varuna River, were idly chatting when one saw a sudden flash of amber under the railway bridge as the girl was set alight. The glow, fierce at first, faded to a flicker, and the fisherman's attention turned back to his friend. The train had passed. All that remained was the skeleton of the iron bridge across the Ganges.

THIRTY-FIVE

Rajveer pulled into the police station, expecting to be able to go home soon. But Arjun had other plans. He had spent the whole journey back in silent thought, the words of the professor playing in his mind.

'Come inside with me. I think I have something.'

'It's late. Can't it wait till the morning? Some of us need our sleep, even if you don't,' replied Rajveer, hesitant to go in, but he had already gone inside.

The first thing he did when he reached the office was flick through the handful of files he had put aside, handing over the file from the basement to Rajveer.

'Take a look at this.'

Rajveer, tired, reluctantly worked her way through the report sheet until she reached the newspaper clipping. The girl's photo looked familiar. The headline read BRIDE'S SUICIDE in VARANASI.

'The girl's name is Savitri – she's a Dalit. Around two years ago, her brothers tried to force her into a marriage, even though she had fallen in love with another man. The brothers refused him as he was from a different caste, and insisted she married the man of their choice. According to the newspaper report, the brothers found the lover and beat him to within an inch of his life. Leaving him for dead in a river, the brothers lied to Savitri and told her he was dead and then forced her to marry a local man. A young girl witnessed Savitri sitting inside her house in full bridal dress as the groom arrived outside. As fireworks were set off outside to celebrate their marriage, Savitri set fire to herself. A few days later, her brothers were found on their own farm, hanged, and the lover just disappeared.'

Rajveer recalled the case. 'I remember it now. We spent weeks looking for the lover based on the witness statement, but we never found him. But what's the connection?'

'Tulsi Vivah – see, it binds Vishnu and Vrinda for eternity in the same way that a Hindu bride and groom walk around the sacred fire seven times to bind themselves forever.'

'The saat phere ritual,' said Rajveer.

'Exactly, and Tulsi plays a very important role. I bet that the killer is forming some kind of bond with the girls before he kills them,' said Arjun, believing it was a significant breakthrough. Rajveer concluded the same.

'My God, he's marrying them!' she said, as she fell back into her seat. Arjun leaned over and said sadly, 'And the poor girl killed herself for love.'

Love was an emotion so powerful that it had turned a sane young man into a monster.

THIRTY-SIX

Sunrise

The elderly man, seated in his chair on the slanting mud bank, was barely conscious. His weary eyes stared across the river. He could just make out the rim of the rising sun lifting above the trees on the opposite bank. He lacked the strength to move his hands in homage to the sun, but his wrinkled cheeks creased a little as he smiled. Slowly his eyes drifted to his right. He'd expected to see his usual morning company, but she was missing.

Helen started the day equally early, making her way to the mission school. With a little more confidence, she rode Agatha's old bike over the wooden slatted footbridge, ascended the bank, and made her way through the trees. She found Bela busy with the children, laying out tables and chairs for the morning class.

'Morning, everyone,' said Helen.

A boat loaded with freshly cut wood arrived and anchored off Manikarnika Ghat. A steady stream of men passed the wood between them until it finally arrived with the woodcutters. Bholadas was among them. He mashed the clay teacup under his sandal and, energised with a burst of sugar-laced tea, he got busy with his axe. He stopped when Arjun arrived. The axe slipped through his hand, his legs gave way beneath him and his heart sank as Arjun broke the news that his daughter's body had been found. The saws and hammers around him fell silent as news spread among the woodcutters. Soon they would be cremating one of their own.

THIRTY-SEVEN

Midday

Rajveer arrived on the outskirts of Savitri's village, thirty kilometres from the city. The road was rough and uneven, and the ride was uncomfortable. As she arrived at the village, the road narrowed, so she stopped. Several villagers crept inside their homes upon seeing her. These were simple folk, unaccustomed to seeing district police officers in their midst. A mother yelled out to her two children, who were blissfully playing in the midday heat: 'Ritu, Shanker, inside, now!' When they didn't respond, she ran out and grabbed them and herded them into her shelter, slamming the door behind her and locking it. The three of them peered through the bars of the door as Rajveer walked past. One by one the doors closed and the alleys emptied: no one wanted to speak to her.

The temple bell chimed. She looked for the temple, thinking there was bound to be a priest inside. A stone statue of Lord Hanuman cast a shadow over the prostrate priest as the sun passed behind it. Rajveer waited until the priest had finished his prayers.

'I'm looking for Laxman Ramdas's house,' she said – the house of Savitri's father. The priest stood up and came outside. He walked halfway around the temple and pointed in the direction she needed to go. As Rajveer walked down the stairs, he spoke to her.

'There's nothing there.'

He was telling the truth: there wasn't much left. The building was charred by fire, the inner rooms covered in a thick coating of dust. All that was visible was a rusty bed frame. The front entrance was boarded up with a crisscross of wooden planks. Rajveer pulled on one and it broke off: they'd become brittle with age. It was a while before she had pulled off enough to enter inside. She found pieces of a broken mirror under the dust, and a half hidden copper pot that had lost its shine. Holding it in her hand, she turned to what was left of the bed, where Savitri had taken her own life.

'There's nothing to find,' a woman's voice shouted out. Rajveer came out to take a look, and found a middle-aged woman sitting outside on the steps of the adjoining house. Her elderly blind mother was by her side and her teenage daughter was tending to her goat. The lady, unlike others in the village, was not afraid to speak to her. As Rajveer came to her, the lady asked her daughter to fetch Rajveer some water.

'Thank you,' Rajveer said to the young girl as she handed her the water.

'Your daughter?'

'Yes, my youngest – my eldest, Bhavna, was Savitri's age when it all happened. Savitri was like a daughter to me. The two of them were best of friends.'

'Can I speak to Bhavna?'

'She's married now – lives far from here. I still can't believe what happened that night.'

'Can you tell me about the man Savitri was in love with?'

'I told the police everything I knew about him at the time.'

'You did? So when did you meet him?'

'No, I didn't say I met him; I never did.'

'Then how did you describe him to the police?'

'Savitri told me what he looked like. I just repeated that to the police officers when they asked about him.'

Rajveer was stunned by the neighbour's revelation. To be sure, she asked again. 'Let's be clear: you never actually met him, right?'

'That's right; that's the truth.'

Quickly, Rajveer returned to her car and sped back to the city.

THIRTY-EIGHT

School over, Helen retreated to the peaceful riverbank. Apart from a few moored fishing boats, riding over the gentle waves, the place was empty. Helen bit into an apple as she continued to turn the pages of the book she had been reading the previous evening. In the light of day, the photos appeared less daunting. She came across a photo of a boy and a priest. The man's hand rested on the child's forehead, holding him still. It reminded her of Nana, and how he held Raju in the forest. She wasn't far from that place; it was only a short stroll downstream beyond the bend of the river. Reading on, she grew curious about the priest's ability to free sinners of guilt. Sarah's death still weighed on her: things could have been different had she not confronted her past and instead kept quiet, as she had done for many years. Sarah would still be alive and Helen would be with her kids back in the classroom, the past buried and silent. But things had happened and changed everything. Sarah's life was her sacrifice, her penance for what she had put Helen through. They both carried guilt.

She turned the page turned and saw a photo of a woman in her twenties bathing in the Ganges. Under it the caption read: *the waters of the Ganges wash away sin.* For a brief moment, Helen saw her own face in place of the woman's, praying and dipping under the water, the water silent and cleansing.

Helen looked downstream. She closed the book and followed the river along the bank and around the bend. She was met by an impassable steep, muddy bank. The only way was to climb up the mud. On her hands and knees she climbed to the forest above. Passing through a thick wall of trees, she came through to the other side. The river flowed below, and beside it was a crumbling shack between two tree stumps. Made from old bricks and covered with forest roots and vines, from a distance it looked like part of the forest. The roof was formed of sheets of rusty metal. The doorway was small. Inside, the space was cramped and the floor made of flattened soil. There was no room to stand upright, and just enough room to take shelter. There was nothing else inside. A wood fire died down in front of the shack. Just then, Helen heard a sound in the water. She leaned over the bank and looked down to see what had caused it.

At the bottom, close to the river, was a funeral pyre, belching smoke as it cooked the corpse of a pauper beneath the flames. A few metres to the right Nana, still in the water, prayed with open arms. Waist-deep in the river, he was naked. His body was coated in a thick muddy clay. Under the roasting sun, the clay cooked and cracked. His eyes opened as Helen stood on a branch, which cracked under her feet.

'This is no place for tourists,' said Nana in polished English, the kind you learn from a private education. He was unmoved by her presence.

'I'm sorry, I didn't mean to intrude.'

'Go away from here – go!'

Helen stepped back, caught her foot on a thick root, and tumbled backwards. She had twisted her ankle; her efforts to get up faltered as the pain was sharp.

Nana climbed out of the river and emerged onto the bank, the thick mud oozed down his body. His crimson cloth hung off a branch, and he pulled it down and tied it round his waist. He had no inhibition, and would have met Helen naked, but he didn't want to frighten her; she was wounded and going nowhere.

When Nana appeared, Helen found herself unable to get up. Clutching her ankle, her pain was visible. Nana knelt down and examined the ankle. The skin was red and swollen. He squeezed it, and she gulped back a sob. He got up and went over to a clay pot that was half-full of water and Tulsi leaves.

'Rest,' he said. She watched as he came back, his hands full of soaked Tulsi. He placed the Tulsi on her sore ankle and pressed it hard.

'It will help with the pain,' said Nana.

His skin was now scarred all over by the dry mud that coated him. He picked up a coconut and cracked it on a stone. Emptying the juice into a shell, he passed it to Helen then tore out the flesh and broke it.

'Thanks. I'm Helen, by the way.'

He didn't reply. Instead he passed her the coconut flesh and then he sat at her side and watched the river. A stray dog crept up behind them and barked. Hungry and frail, it was barely alive, still it had the energy to bark. It appeared to be troubled by Nana.

Nana picked up his staff and taunted it. The dog bit the tip of the stick and wrestled with it until it had exhausted its strength, then it left, defeated.

'Don't let it bother you. The dog's troubled by the burning body. There are those who believe dogs see the souls of the departing – you'll find many dogs barking on the ghats. Listen to them, the barking – they see what others do not: a city of souls rising from the ashes. Does it not trouble you to be so close to death?' he asked Helen.

It should have bothered her, but the few days she'd been in Varanasi had already changed her. She seemed less troubled by the presence of corpses and funeral pyres. She surprised him.

'No, it doesn't. Is that what you do – burn bodies?'

Nana looked straight at her. He rarely engaged in conversation and never with foreigners, but she interested him: she seemed unafraid; someone to study. In his earlier life, Nana had loved to study. A graduate of New Delhi University, he came from a middle-class family. Both parents were engineers, with a house and car, and he their pride and joy. He had everything he wanted: a girlfriend, money, an education and a job lined up – everything for the taking. But visiting Varanasi had turned the middle-class graduate into a wandering nomad. Aged twenty-three, he arrived on the ghats for a short stopover with three friends. They had ridden down on their Royal Enfield motorbikes from the ancient mountain city Leh in north-west India and followed the Ganges east through the holy city of Rishikesh and downriver to Banaras.

When he had arrived he found a city struggling to find its way, torn between its present and sacred past. But it was when he wandered alone in the forest beyond the city, by the Varuna River, that his life had changed forever. Here, at this very spot, he had arrived – like Helen – and met a stranger in the water. He had stayed with the stranger overnight as a corpse burned on a small fire. Nearby, the two challenged one another's understanding of the world around them, until they retired for the night. However, the stranger did not sleep. In early hours, as the fire burned down, the corpse was half-burned, its flesh still on the bone, charred and tough. Nana was woken by a dog barking. He opened his eye but remained still. At the pyre he saw the stranger take pieces of the corpse from the fire and feast upon it. Tearing at the charred flesh, his mouth full, he swallowed. Each bite fuelled him: it was the person's soul he was consuming. This was one of thousands he'd claimed in order to build his strength: he believed that with each soul he grew more powerful, a god in the making. And when he was dead, another would feast upon him, passing the souls of thousands from one life to another, and on it would go – a journey that had begun a thousand years before, when the first soul was taken.

The stranger knew he was being watched, and waited to be stopped, but Nana said nothing. The stranger held all the power: the strength to do as he pleased, without fear, without emotion.

When Nana woke, he found the stranger had left, but he'd left him a message. Carved inside the inner shell of a coconut, it read: *To have nothing, is everything.* Nana went back to his hotel and returned to Delhi. The stranger's words stayed with him: he learned more about the strange men of Banaras, and the more he read, the closer he came to understanding them. Within a year he'd arrived back in Banaras, leaving behind his perfect girlfriend and mapped-out life. Instead he embraced the stranger's life and took his place on the cremation ground. His parents eventually tracked him down, finding him half-starved and shivering in a stinging cold December fog, but he refused to return. He'd come too far – he had to break with all material things. That included his family and their love for him. Only then would he be free from everything.

That morning he promised his parents he would return to see them at the hotel they were staying at – a five-star hotel in the old cantonment area of the city, where colonial buildings formed a line of hotels and wealthy homes. Nana kept his promise. Arriving on time in the hotel's lobby, in a robe. He threw the robe off as his parents came to greet him. He never felt his mother's embrace – she didn't recognise him at first, but then, as the shock passed, she saw her boy's eyes. The rest was just a naked man, covered in a corpse's ash from the neck down, and a dead dog wrapped around his waist. Its smell sprang out and hit her. She screamed and fainted. His efforts paid off: he wanted to break all bonds and emotional attachments with his parents and his bold act achieved this. They were so sickened by their son, they never came back for him again. Like the stranger had before him, he found his freedom in the solace of the river, and being free to do as he pleased.

'They've been burning bodies here long before I came here. It's a peaceful place for it, not like the city. The villagers from near and far bring me their dead, and I take what I need from the forest and build a fire to cremate the bodies. Some pay me, some don't. Some give food. I ask for nothing – just to be alone.'

'You live here?' she asked, sipping the coconut juice.

Nana saw Helen's shoulder bag on the grass, the book half out, and the cover drew his attention. He picked it up.

'The Aghori.'

'Why do they look so different?' Helen asked.

'Different? To them, perhaps, you are different. They look that way to separate themselves from others. They're not bad; they follow old ways.'

The birds crowed in the trees. The forest was coming to life as the sun set to end the day.

'This is not your first time here, is it?'

'I've never been here before. It's my first time in India.' Helen found his assumption amusing.

'How would you know for sure? Not in this life, but in a past one, you've been here.'

'You mean reincarnation. I don't think so.'

'Hindus believe in life after death, and rebirth and death again, and on it goes.' His words seemed tortured.

'One life's enough for me.' Helen's voice softened. She lowered her eyes, glazed with pain, remembering.

'The Aghori, they're not so different from you. They're also tired of this life after life: they want to end it.' Nana held her with his eyes. 'They want moksha.'

'Moksha?'

'No more life, no more death – to be free for eternity.' He saw a change in Helen; she was getting weary. Although his eyes still held her, she drifted in his words. He used this to his advantage and weaved his words with subtle suggestions, like a master hypnotist, his hold over her growing. She didn't know it, but she was no longer in control.

'What price would you pay to be free, Helen?'

She swayed, her head grew dizzy, and the coconut shell fell from her grasp. Her eyes followed his. Bound together, she was his.

'I... I...' She struggled to find words. She remembered a little more. 'I...'

'Why are you here?' By now his voice was just a blur. She tried to find the words that were buried deep inside her.

'I'm not sure... I'm feeling.'

Nana kept quiet, waiting for her words.

'My... my... my father,' she said, her head heavy.

'Your father, Helen. Tell me about your father.'

'My father... he...' she trailed off.

'Your father – he hurt you, Helen.'

She disagreed but couldn't say so.

'He hurt you, didn't he?'

'My father, my father.' Her words slowed. drained, her head slumped. Nana put his hand on her head and held her. She fell into a deep sleep as the forest awoke.

THIRTY-NINE

Evening

Arjun pinned a black-and-white cut-out of Savitri's photo, reprinted from the newspaper article clipped in the file, to his board. Her face joined the faces of the four girls burned to death, and the woodcutter's daughter.

'She lied to the neighbour about her lover's appearance,' said Rajveer.

'But why would she do that?' he questioned.

'To protect him – don't you see? This way he could stay close to her without anyone suspecting anything. Even if her brothers found out about him from neighbours, they'd end up looking for someone else. I guess his luck ran out – they found him, beat him up and left him for dead.'

Arjun pulled out the file and scanned through the articles. He pinned up the text he was looking for. The article included several rumours that had been doing the rounds at the time of her suicide. A local farmer reported he'd been with the two brothers when they were drunk, and heard them boasting that they'd taken care of an outsider who'd dishonoured their sister.

The truth was that Savitri's brothers had given Kasi a severe beating, thrashing him with their sticks until he collapsed. Even then, they had continued to beat him until they had exhausted their anger. And when they were done, they rolled Kasi's broken body into the river, and watched as the current carried him out of sight.

What they didn't realise was, a few hundred metres downriver, Kasi had washed up onto the riverbank, where he'd lain on the dirt for a day and half, unnoticed. His face was swollen and covered in blood, and he repeated one word, over and over: *Savitri*. The only thing that kept Kasi alive was the thought of seeing her once more.

'Excuse me, mam.' Tripathi arrived with a list of local employers, mainly textile manufacturers. Arjun had asked Tripathi earlier to find out where Savitri had previously worked. It crossed his mind that perhaps she had met her boyfriend at work. It was another avenue he wanted to explore. The jobs had all been in admin, back to back for four years, all in the same area, with barely a week between one employer and the next. Then a gap appeared: eleven months between her last two employers. Her last job had been with a local travel agent. But the job before she took the break was working for a small garment factory, Trivedi Exports. The company was located within a cluster of textile workshops on the eastern side of the old city.

'I know the area well. I'll look into it,' said Rajveer, taking the list from Arjun.

'Find out what you can. She'd worked there close to a year, so someone there must have an idea of why she left.'

FORTY

Night

The fire spat and crackled under the watchful eyes of crows nestled between the branches. A cobra hissed nearby. Helen was still asleep, her cheek against the worn grass. As a beetle crawled into her ear, she snapped upright, as though she'd woken from a terrible dream. Her breathing was heavy and panicked. The crows burst out from the treetops.

Nana sat in front of her, beyond the fire, his back to her. He looked up to the sky – never had he seen so many stars glitter in one night. He knew she was awake. He picked up a loose stone and looked across the river, which was calm and reflected the sparkling stars.

'A perfect night,' he said, as he threw the stone into the water. 'Each night the universe is destroyed as the maker sleeps, and reborn each morning as the maker awakens.'

The ripples spread out then flattened, the water calmed and the stars returned.

'I am but a philosopher trapped in the mind of a wandering beggar who lives among the souls of the dead, rather than the living. Am I so different?' He turned to Helen, looking over his shoulder.

'How long I have been here?' she asked, still dazed from her heavy sleep.

'As long as you needed,' Nana replied. Turning back to the river, he dipped both hands in the water pot in front of him. It contained a mix of freshly picked local herbs and leaves. He cupped the water in his closed hands and caressed his face.

She felt uneasy in the darkness. Agatha came to her mind; she must be worried. Her swollen ankle felt better. She got up and found she could walk.

'It's late, I should go.'

Still Nana kept his back to her. Covering his skin with the oiled water, he raised what was left in the pot and poured it over his hair, inhaling the scent as the water drained down his face. Helen left, but before she was out of sight, Nana spoke.

'You know where to find me when you need me.'

She stopped and turned at his words – he was so sure she would return. He was barely visible between the trees. She turned and found the dog in front of her. It was the one from earlier. It barked at her, calling her. The trees all appeared the same in the dark; she knew she had to go upstream along the river, and that was where the dog was heading. She followed it.

After a short stroll through the dense shrubs, the river reappeared. She could see the faint lights of the village. This is where she and the dog parted company. She headed out into the village as the dog looked on, disinclined to go any further. When she looked back, the dog had vanished.

FORTY-ONE

Night

LORD OF CHAI, read the neon sign. The word 'Chai' flickered as the current failed to pass through it. It hung above a small teashop that sprawled by the edge of the road, with cheap plastic tables filled with snacks laced with oil and chutneys. The haunt was a local for police, as it sat directly opposite the station. It fed night workers and street dwellers who had a few rupees to cover the cost of piping hot tea and a spicy vegetable-filled dough, tossed and crisped in sizzling oil.

The chef, in torn jeans and a T-shirt, flicked fresh oil onto a large frying pan. He cracked three eggs into it with one hand and stirred the teapot as it frothed to the rim with the other.

'One tea,' Kasi ordered, then pulled out five small clear glasses from the water pot, which had been soaked to clean, and lined them up in a row.

'Two teas.' Arjun placed his order> he was standing at Kasi's side. He looked at him with a polite smile. The chef poured tea into all five glasses, with two extra ready for taking. Arjun took the tea and sat next to Rajveer on a wooden bench. The nightly news broadcast played on the radio, reporting on the body found at the farm.

Arjun took out a cigarette and his box of matches, which was empty. A hand extended towards him, holding a lighter, and lit his cigarette for him.

'Thanks,' said Arjun, noticing in passing the green stone ring on Kasi's finger.

'No problem,' replied Kasi he took his tea and sat at the end of the same bench, looking away to the other side. Rajveer was barely a foot away from him. Kasi flicked through his phone, his face lit up by the light from the screen.

'The future of India,' Arjun remarked, joking about a generation of mobile phone addicts.

'No doubt texting his girlfriend.'

'How about you?' he asked Rajveer, who was a little surprised by the question.

'Me? I'm… what do they say, married to the job. How about you? Is there a Mrs Das back in Delhi?'

'No.' he laughed. 'Plenty of women in the past, but the work – it kind of has a hold on you. You think you can leave the office and it stays there, but it doesn't; it creeps back in. I never notice it; it's always someone else. They find me lost in thought at the dinner table, losing my train of thought halfway through a conversation, sweating in the night. How can I share my life with someone when I keep so many secrets?'

Arjun ordered another glass of tea. A police jeep left the station, its sirens on and red lights flashing. The tea arrived, steaming.

'Why did you leave Varanasi?' asked Rajveer. Arjun held the warm teacup close to his nose and sniffed at the infused steam.

'I felt suffocated. After my parents died, there was nothing left to keep me here. I knew if I stayed I would never amount to much, so I packed up and bought a one-way train ticket to Delhi. I took on any work I could find in the day, and studied at night, and finally arrived at the CBI.'

He looked at Rajveer, who shied away from eye contact.

'You understand,' he said.

'What do you mean?'

'Come on – that story of Firozpur, your military family? It's a wonderful story, but it's just that – a story.' Arjun seemed to be forcing Rajveer to think about something that was buried deep inside her.

'Give me some credit. We're not so different, are we?'

'If you know it all, why bring it up?' She struggled to say more, like a child who's been caught lying. Arjun held back, giving her space to come back in her own time. She looked at Kasi, who had earphones on, and the remaining customers were far enough away not to overhear. Rajveer turned back to Arjun.

'A five-year-old girl goes to school for the first time. What does she expect? To study, to play, to have fun. Her mother holds her hand all the way to the entrance, and tells her to do exactly as the teachers say – they are like gurus and should be obeyed. So the girl went to take the teacher's hand, but he never took it. Instead he told her to sit at the back of the class, away from the other children. During the break everyone goes out to have their lunch, to run around, and then they come back into the class. This girl was not allowed in.'

Arjun lowered his eyes. Her story reminded him of his own time at school.

'She was sent to the toilet, to clean it. At the end of the day she went back to her father and cried, and when she asked why they had treated her like this, her father just told her, that's how it is.'

'So you grew up and ran away? Invented a new life story?' said Arjun.

'Sunita Chandra Ram became Rajveer Saxsena, the girl from Firozpur.'

'And no one else knows?' he asked.

Rajveer shook her head. 'I'd like to keep it that way,' she said. The truth, if people found out, would cost her everything.

He looked at her with a sigh of pity. Unlike him, she was still living in the shadow of her past. Under her tough exterior, the tears of that five-year-old girl were still there. She was scarred under her skin, a constant reminder when she looked into the mirror that she was still her father's girl.

Arjun extended his hand. 'I don't believe we've been introduced,' he said. 'I'm Arjun.'

She smiled and shook his hand. 'Hi, I'm Sunita.'

'Nice to meet you, Sunita.'

Behind Rajveer, Kasi was ready to leave. He neatly folded his headphones into his pocket. He walked to the chef and settled his bill. He handed him a 100-rupee note and waited for change. It gave him a few seconds to look back at them both, sitting at the bench. A part of him was left wanting – it was all too easy. Here he was, so close to the law, briskly going about his business, a fox in the lion's den, and they were busy with tea and small talk, while the fox watched from the sidelines. Should he stay and tease them, or walk away?

'Sir, sir.' The cook's voice rose a little as Kasi failed to take his change. Arjun turned around to take a look, and found Kasi watching at him with a taunting stare. Kasi tore his eyes away, grabbed his change and walked away. His work was not yet done.

FORTY-TWO

A small group of university students, young men in their twenties, having escaped their dorms, raced along the river bank, lighting cigarettes as they ran. One of them carried a plastic bag, inside which rattled bottles of cheap beer.

They came across an empty wooden boat, moored on the mud, far from the water. There was a reason for this: cut into its side was a large hole. The students sat in the boat, opened the beer bottles and shared the beer between them. Far from home, the students came from Mumbai, Delhi and Bangalore – cities far larger than Varanasi, and more liberal in their living.

The railway bridge branched out above them. As they sat and drank, the playing cards came out and the chatter flowed. A girl, Asha, that one of them had taken a fancy to, became the centre of their banter. The cards laid out, they clinked their bottles together in a toast to freedom, to girls, and to Asha.

The shouting stopped as an object turned and drifted from the river and onto the silt. The Ganges water batted it back and forth in the current, but the object was stuck. 'Is that... a dead body?' said one young man, leaning over to look, but staying in the comfort of the boat.

'Yeah, it looks like it,' said another.

'Salu, get rid of it,' said one to another. Salu was the most masculine among them, boastful of his strength. He stalled at first, but the others cheered him on: 'Salu, Salu, Salu!' He grabbed his friend's bottle and downed it in one, then picked up the wooden oar from inside the boat and made his way down to the object. He approached with caution but, aware that his friends were watching him, he buried any hesitation. A ragged cloth clung around the object; he prodded it with the oar. It was nothing more than a rotted lump of wood, covered in torn cloth, and a shaft of splintered bark held it in the silt.

'Is it a body?' came from behind him.

'It is,' he said, playing along with them. The students calmed, their jeers silenced.

'What should I do?' he asked. 'It looks like the rib cage.'

His friend choked at the thought. 'Push it back into the water.'

Locals often complained about finding parts of corpses washing up, half burned and rotting. Usually they were the remains of a cheap cremation, when less firewood was used – and when it burned out, anything that remained was pushed into the water.

Salu placed the oar under the wood and flipped it hard towards the boat.

His friends all cried out as they threw themselves out of the boat as the wood landed inside. All they could hear was Salu laughing. They peered inside and found no corpse.

Close by, a fat rat kept watch from inside the cave under the bridge. As the students continued to play cards and drink, behind them, a pack of rats feasted in the dark.

FORTY-THREE

Crouched in a corner, Kasi rolled a joint, struck a light and lay back, exhaling as he did so, releasing the stress he held within himself. He rolled his neck, and the bones cracked. The footprints of a gecko left marks as it sprinted across the mirror in front of him. From his pocket Kasi pulled out his phone, put it on speaker, and tapped the play button.

'Come on – that story of Firozpur, your military family?' It was Arjun's voice. Kasi had recorded their conversation. He hadn't been listening to music; he was listening to them. The recording played on. He inhaled and felt a little numb.

'Savitri... Savitri,' he said gently. As the ganja worked its magic, he found himself lured into his past.

Two years earlier, Kasi and Savitri, bound by a holy thread, had walked around a sacred fire inside a temple ruin. A voice from outside had recited the vows, and they had repeated each verse as they completed a circle around the fire. They had said vow after vow until all seven were done, and then Savitri had placed a garland over Kasi and he had placed his own over her. The sacred fire was witness to their union. Savitri had placed a ring on his finger. It bore a dullish green stone, and was of little value; she'd picked it up from a market stall. For her, though, it was more than a stone: it was a bond, a promise to be with one another. A cheap stone ring: worth nothing, worth everything.

The ring in place, the two were one, husband and wife, in the eyes of God. Nothing could change that. She held him firmly, his strength hers. She needed it. Her brothers would not be so easy to please. Kasi held her hands, and felt them shake.

'You're mine now; I will deal with your brothers.'

Kasi felt her grip on his back. He felt hot, feverish. He cried out: 'Savitri!'

He was back in his den, shivering, haunted by his memories. He saw his face in the mirror. The heat still burned. His eyes twitched. He could hear her cries: 'Kasi... Kasi!'

He covered his ears and cried out. Her screams became unbearable. He saw the fire engulf the mirror: he saw her in the glass, on fire.

'Ahhhhh,' he cried, smashing the mirror with his hands. A shard sliced through his hand.

Exhausted, he fell back, his cries silenced. The gecko appeared again, clinging to the ceiling above him. Its bulging eyes looked down on him.

His right hand bled, and he let it.

FORTY-FOUR

Dawn

A stray dog licked Salu's fingers as he rested inside the boat, his hand over the edge. He felt the dog's moist tongue. 'Shit,' he said, shooing the dog away. It didn't go far, as it found a dried-up fish to eat. Now he was up, burdened by his heavy consumption of beer, he found he needed a piss. He looked around for an empty beer bottle and found one. As he picked it up, the cave's opening caught his eye. It was a private space. He stepped up to the entrance and unzipped himself. About to urinate, he suddenly stopped. A terrible smell forced him to cover his mouth. He heard a noise coming from inside the cave; it was the rats, scurrying around out of sight. He pulled out a match and struck it, briefly lighting the old stone walls and rubbish on the ground.

'Fuck me.'

He stumbled backwards and raced out of the cave and back to the boat. Terrified, he woke the others.

Morning

The train passengers' tempers flared – they'd been stationary for two hours. The main station was barely a mile away on the other side of the railway bridge. The cause of the delay was not known to them, but the train driver could see, through the bridge, several police officers. They were examining the tracks above the cave, watched by a crowd of local fishermen and residents of Raj Ghat. Police jeeps and an ambulance had parked on the road above; below, inside the cave, the entrance was guarded by two officers. Outside on the riverbank the students were lined up, their names and details being taken down. Rats scavenged along the old wall that ran parallel to the cave, desperately seeking a new home as they were forced to abandon their current one.

Crouched on the ground, amidst the debris of broken beer glasses and crushed bricks, Rajveer, her mouth covered by a cloth, wearing forensic gloves, picked through the detritus, looking for anything that's seemed to be out of place.

'What kind of man could do this,' she muttered under the cloth.

Arjun knelt beside a burned corpse. Less bothered by the smell, he glided the torch inches above the scorched flesh and bone, as crisp and sticky as tar. He kept quiet as he observed the body closely. The torch funnelled its light to form a circle; his eyes followed it across the corpse's head. The skin had gone, the eye sockets empty, the scalp crusted. The mouth was open, the jaw and teeth naked and black. The torch moved down to the neck, and the body curled up beneath it. The corpse was on its side; what remained of the arms melted into one another behind it, where the hands were bound.

Rajveer leaned over and spotted something.

'That – go back,' she said, pointing to the corpse's wrist. Arjun shone his torch over it.

The burned flesh was torn and split by the feasting rats, the bone underneath clearly visible. At the base of the wrist was a piece of copper, oxidized in the fire, that had survived. Arjun picked off the ash, and rubbed it. Letters appeared one after another.

'M ... A ... Y ... A.'

Arjun stumbled back, gasping.

'What is it?' Rajveer asked.

'Maya,' he replied. 'Maya.' He looked at her faceless head.

'You knew her?'

'She was a friend.'

'I'm sorry.'

'Sir,' Tripathi called, his body silhouetted at the entrance to the cave. He had a plastic bag in his hand. Arjun appeared and gasped for air. Shaken by Maya's death, he left it to Rajveer to take a look. She found a bushel of Tulsi leaves inside. The bag had been found close by, nailed into the rising bank above the wall, a signpost left for the taking.

Arjun gazed across the bridge, his eyes straying down the ribbon of ghats that lined the banks of the old city. Kasi had finally left his calling card: the Tulsi in the bag had been left not by accident, but by choice.

'He's here, in the city, and he's sending us a message. He's not afraid of us – of anyone.' Arjun looked at Rajveer. 'He's already looking for his next victim.'

And he was right. Kasi was on the ghats, barely a kilometre upstream, chilling out under a stone arch, playing his guitar, teasing a group of unsuspecting girls, who were happy to be charmed. As they gossiped and played along, there was one girl in particular who caught his eye. She looked down shyly as he smiled at her. Her name was Gita, and she was a local garland-seller.

FORTY-FIVE

Midday

The children gathered inside the mission's chapel. It was too small to hold them all, and they, along with well-wishers, spilled out into the courtyard. In the silence they heard Agatha read out a letter written by Raju.

I was only five when you came into my life. You brought me joy and happiness and taught me how to smile. You were my sister, my teacher, my best friend. You were everything.

The children were led one by one, by the hand, to light a candle and place it in front of Maya's photo. Agatha held Maya's sister Chaya as the children filed past. Outside, Arjun waited for Helen. She had been the last person to see Maya – that he knew of. As the vigil came to a close, Helen came outside, and found Arjun talking to a missionary sister.

'Hi,' she said with a soft politeness.

'Excuse me,' he said to the sister.

'How is she holding up?' he asked, referring to Agatha.

'She's holding up. She has to, for the children's sake. How about you? Maya was your friend.'

They sat on the bench under the veranda.

'I'll mourn her when this over. Right now I just want to find the man who did this and….' He wanted to kill him. He didn't have to utter the words; his eyes said it all.

'I understand you were with Maya all day in the ghats and markets?'

'That's right, but we went our own ways at the end of the day. The last I saw of her was when she ran towards a bus.'

'Did you see her get in?' he asked

'No, no I didn't. I'd left in a rickshaw by then.'

'Do you remember anything strange happening in the day? Anyone, anything out of place?'

'I don't think so. We just walked around the stalls and riverside, shared stories and.... she made me feel happier than I've been for a while. She was so warm and kind. I barely knew her, but anyone could see how devoted she was to the children. It's impossible to understand why anyone would want to harm her.'

'This place, like any other, has its demons.'

Helen fell silent.

'Please, I need you to go over that day, over and over, think about where you went, who you saw, what time it was, what you bought, who spoke to you – anything. Just write it all down, it doesn't matter how irrelevant you think it is. I'll come over tomorrow and we can run through it.'

FORTY-SIX

Textile Workshop

A box of condoms vibrated on the plinth that was fixed to the side of a handloom as the shuttle passed through a ray of saffron threads. The weaver, a teenager, pushed the pedal hard, keeping time with his fingers and eyes, as the threads wove in and out to form a silk cloth. The clunking and spinning of endless looms made talking difficult. The weavers' workshop was crammed and dark, with bare light bulbs dangling from above and old and young, fathers and sons, busy weaving. A weaver stopped as the shuttle got caught between the threads. He reached into the box. Shuttle in hand, he rubbed a condom over it, to lubricate it. Now oiled, he placed it back and as he applied the pedal, the shuttle flew and the chunking continued again.

Rajveer parked outside the workshop. The hand-painted board saying *Trivedi Exports* matched the name on the police file. Inside she made her way past the looms, and a weaver directed her to the room at the back. It had a window, and plenty of natural light, unlike the workshop. It was the manager's office, Mr Altar.

She had to knock several times to catch his attention. He was a plump man who had spent years shouting over the weavers' noise, so that his own hearing had suffered. He was buried in his ledger, checking a sales order, when Rajveer entered, having giving up knocking. She tapped him on the shoulder. At first he was surprised by her sudden presence. His glasses, barely resting on the tip of his nose, fell off, but were held by the string around his neck. Rajveer flashed her badge and as usual, said nothing at first, just sized him up from head to toe, and wandered across to the files and stacks of rolled-up silks. It was her way of taking control. She looked out of the window. The workers had slowed their pace and avoided eye contact with her. She closed the door to escape the noise. That did little to dampen the noise, and she had to raise her voice to be heard. Mr

Altar cleaned his glasses with a cloth before putting them back on. They got down to discussing his former employee.

'She was the best assistant I had – always the first one in and last to leave. I felt sick when I read about her death in the papers.'

'Was she close to anyone who worked here?'

'She was friendly to everyone, but if you mean anything more, no, not to my knowledge.'

'And you never saw her lover.'

'No.'

'When she decided to leave her job, did she give you a reason why?'

He thought about it, then pulled out an old ledger from his cabinet and ran his fingers through the pages until he came to some notes he'd made on a specific day.

'Allahabad,' he said. 'She was going there to study. I offered to pay for a local course but she insisted – her mind was made up.'

Rajveer scribbled it down. 'Do you know which college?'

He had no reply. 'I heard she'd come back after a while, but she never came here, and I never saw her again. So sad what happened to her.'

Midday

'Sir, lunch,' said the tea boy as he caught his breath, having run from the snack bar in an effort to deliver the food hot. He'd brought a spiced grilled potato-and-pea sandwich, wrapped in a newspaper, and a small plastic pouch with fresh tea inside. Arjun had deliberately over-ordered. He took half and passed the rest back to the boy, along with a tip.

'Salam, sir.' The boy thanked him with a genuine smile. Rarely, if ever, had he been treated so nicely – to have an officer of the CBI share his food with him was a great honour.

But before Arjun could take a bite, his mobile rang. He answered. It was CBI Assistant Director Singh. Having received the news of Maya's death, he was under pressure from the Justice Ministry for immediate action, as the press were beginning to ask difficult questions.

'My neck is on the line,' he said. 'I personally vouched for you – and now this.'

'And I won't let you down. I'm sure we're on the right track with this bride's suicide.'

The phone on the desk rang and rang. An officer answered from the other side as he saw Arjun was busy on the other phone. It was Rajveer.

'Just throw everything you have at it,' said Singh, and with distaste he continued: 'Mehra called – gave me an earful about your inability to stop the killings, wanted me to recall you. I won't give him the benefit, but if there's another death, I will have to, you understand?'

The phone call ended. Tempted to call back, Arjun put his finger on the dial but refrained from pushing the buttons. He knew the situation was coming to a climax, but he held back. Sharing this would only add to the pressure.

'Sir, madam called.' The officer passed him a note. Rajveer was on her way to Allahabad, rather than return to the office. The city was only a few hours' drive down the main highway. She had also asked the officers to make a list of all the colleges in Allahabad and check to see if Savitri had attended any of them during the months she was there.

FORTY-SEVEN

Night

Rajveer arrived outside a grimy one-star hotel, a few streets downtown from the local police station. She'd been sent there by the local police station, which had an informal arrangement with the hotel's manager. He ran a brothel on the top three floors, but kept the ground and first floor for paying guests – and, on occasion, for off-duty police officers, who stayed for free. It netted the police station's chief a tidy share of the profits each month from the brothel's takings. At the reception desk, the manager, in slacks and a colourful shirt, eyed up Rajveer. She was the first female police officer to be sent here. He wondered if she was lost at first, but when she showed him the note from the police chief, he gave her a room. He walked her to the first floor, up a narrow set of steps. As they climbed the stairs, the sound of music and women giggling got louder, along with drunken men occasionally calling out prostitutes' names.

He opened the room door for her, and she took the keys. The manager kept his foot in the door as she went to close it.

'Is there anything else you need? I was about to order some food, and I can order for two,' the manager said, thinking himself in with a chance. She put her hand to her side, where her gun was buckled.

'Right. Just leave the keys on the desk when you leave in the morning.' He left.

She went over to the window, which was filthy. The wood was chipped around the frame, and a draught blew in, along with the smell of burning oil from the food stalls outside. The torn curtain barely covered half the window and, even where it did, the cloth was thin and transparent. Her phone rang. Arjun's name appeared on the screen.

'We've managed to narrow it down to five colleges – all had students named Savitri during the same period. I've sent over an ID photo to each of them, so we'll know by morning if there is any direct match.'

'Thanks. Listen, my phone might go dead, the battery's almost out, so in case you can't get me leave a note at reception.' She gave the name of the hotel and its number from the sticker on the room phone.

'I'll check in with Helen in the morning, to run through what she remembers.' As he spoke, a pounding sound came from above. She looked up and noticed the lampshade swaying.

'Hello... Rajveer, hello?'

'Shit,' she said. There was no way she was going to sleep under that all night.

'Everything OK?' he asked.

'Yes, fine. I'll speak to you in the morning.'

She went into the bathroom and washed her face, but even in there she couldn't escape the mischief happening above.

'Shit, shit, shit,' she shouted, then left the room and went straight down the stairs, where the manager tried to keep a straight face as it dawned on her what was happening upstairs. Before she shouted him down, an off-duty police officer appeared at the stop of the steps, shirt undone. Clearly drunk, he demanded another bottle of whisky be sent up. It dawned on her that the place was protected.

'Oy,' she called to the manager as he rummaged under the desk to pull out a bottle of local whisky.

'Do you have a phone charger for this?' She showed him her phone. He didn't.

'I'm expecting a call from Varanasi in the morning. Make sure you write down what they say.'

'Sure,' he said. 'You're not staying?' he said, leaning over the desk as Rajveer walked out. She parked the police jeep under a streetlight next to a small line of street stalls. It was going to be a rough night.

FORTY-EIGHT

Night

An unexpected storm blew in from the north, and with it a strong breeze. The rain danced on the stone pavements. Inside her room, Helen wrestled with her demons. The screams of her innocence echoed and tortured her. Her eyes twitched as her pupils moved violently under her eyelids, as she remembered.

She felt the grip around her throat, being unable to breathe. Then her tormentor appeared.

'No… no,' she cried, tears leaking from her eyes.

'No,' she tossed from side to side. 'No!' Her cries got louder. Agatha, who had been woken by the rain, heard her too.

'No! No, Dad, no, please, Dad, no,' she pleaded as her throat choked. 'No! Dad, no, leave me alone, Dad.'

Agatha stood, stunned, on the other side of the door.

'My God,' she said. 'Helen?' She came to her side.

'Dad, please don't touch me, don't touch me,' Helen cried.

'Helen, what did he do to you? Helen, wake up.' She shook her, but Helen was trapped inside her nightmare.

Agatha grabbed a cloth from the table, wet it in the water bowl, and placed it on Helen's feverish head. The cold water calmed her. Her eyes slowly opened. In front of her, holding her hands, was Agatha.

'My child, I'm sorry, I'm so sorry. What did he do to you? Tell me, Helen. I'm here for you.'

'I can't, I...' Helen wanted to say it, but she remembered Sarah – the truth had already claimed her mother, and she didn't want to hurt anyone else.

'Helen, listen to me. I heard everything. He hurt you, didn't he? He really hurt you.'

'No. I just want to be alone.'

'Listen to me. I-I-I wasn't myself back then, after David died. I didn't know what to do; I just wanted to get away from it all.' Agatha embraced her.

'What are you saying?' Helen cried on Agatha's shoulder.

'I wanted to tell you when I first saw you. I-I'm your mother, Helen. I'm your mother, not Sarah.'

Helen broke off, confused and shocked by Agatha's revelation.

'That's not possible – why are you saying that? Why?'

'Because it's the truth – it's the truth. That's why Sarah left you the pendant. She knew you'd bring it to me: she was sending you back to me. I'm so sorry.'

'No, no... All these years, she would have told me and Jack...'

'David was your father – David.' Agatha tried to hold Helen's hand as she trembled and cried.

'Forgive me, Helen. I beg you to forgive me.'

'All these years! No, it's not possible.'

'Forgive me, but what did he do to you, Helen? What did he do?'

'He... he raped me, he raped me.' Agatha's legs gave way. Helen, nauseated and confused, ran outside into the chill rain and out of the mission. A few street lights sprinkled light along the narrow alley on both sides, and the potholes were filled with rainwater. She stopped and sank down to the steps, her vest and cotton pyjama pants soaked through. Agatha's confession filled her thoughts – Agatha was her mother! The pieces fitted: the pendant, her father's anger towards her, the rape – she wasn't his child – and Sarah's last letter.

By the time Agatha arrived outside, Helen was gone, the alley empty. The rain had slowed to a steady tap. Helen had walked to the footbridge. A couple of metres to one side, above the bank a shack provided comfort to a few villagers. Tea was on the boil on a makeshift stove. An elderly gentlemen, draped in a blanket, stared at her. The footbridge was barely visible. She approached the man. Pitying her – she was a foreigner, either lost or mad to roam around at this late hour – he lit her a fire torch. She stepped onto the bridge, held the ropes and made her way across the slippery slats as the man watched from the shack. She made it to the other side and climbed up the bank.

The footpath vanished as the muddy track turned into shrubs and grass. Helen walked past the mission school and continued through the forest, being showered by raindrops falling from the branches above her until she came to a camp fire.

'Don't be afraid,' said Nana, standing behind her.

FORTY-NINE

Night

Helen sheltered inside Nana's shack while Nana rekindled the fire outside. Helen warmed her numb skin as Nana tended the fire until they both felt the flames. She waited for him to ask her why she was there, but he sat there saying nothing, poking a twig into a coconut he'd placed inside the fire.

'I don't know why I'm here.' They were her first words after arriving. He still said nothing.

The silence eased her breathing. She felt less tense: as he demanded nothing from her, she felt at home. A few minutes passed as the coconut charred and smoked, and when it was ready Nana used his stick to push it out of the flames and crack it open. He scraped out the roasted flesh into two shells and passed one to Helen. Along with the juice of another, she slaked her thirst and shared the nutty aroma of the coconut.

He smiled as she ate; she felt disarmed and unafraid. And when they were finished eating, he extended his hands and she held them.

'It's time.' Her fingers gripped his, his eyes drew hers, his breath became hers.

'Shhh,' he whispered. 'Shhh.'

'I-I-I'm feeling a little dizzy… I can't see clearly,' Helen faltered.

Nana said nothing as he looked into her eyes.

'Shhh,' was all he said.

'I, I…'

He leaned over and placed his forehead against hers, and ran his fingers through her hair

'Shhh.' He inhaled, she exhaled, the two of them as one.

'Let yourself go, set yourself free… let it go.'

There was no magic at play, no drugs; just his voice and touch. Nana had mastered the art of hypnosis, fine-tuned it in the quiet of the forest where he preyed on unsuspecting wanderers. At first he emptied Helen's mind into a pool of darkness: in the distance, a flame danced, and the river's ripples appeared to glow. Helen found herself inside a wooden fishing boat as they broke through the ripples. The fisherman's oar cut through the water. The boat was steered by Nana, who sat behind her, his legs crossed. She didn't turn to look at him; instead, her focus remained on the light as it drew closer. His voice breathed past her.

'I will set you free.'

The boat passed an old temple, partly submerged in the water. A lonely girl sat inside, above the river's shine, her face lit by a fire. Helen recognised her: she had her eyes, her hair, her childhood face. She sat, silent in fear, and the boat rowed past. The light died and a shiver rippled down her spine as she found herself unable to distinguish anything in the darkness above or below her. Without warning, Nana capsized the boat, and they both fell into the river. Helen sank, pulled down by Nana's hands, tugging at her ankles. Darkness swirled around her, her breath escaped: she was ready to surrender, then his voice came to her: 'Free yourself, Helen. Free yourself… free yourself.'

Her lungs closed, her hands scrabbled in the water as she kicked and freed herself. Bursting through the river into the air, she gasped and filled her lungs with fresh air. The sky above her filled with starlight, the moon full and bold, cut a perfect circle as the moonshine drifted over her. She crawled out onto the riverbank, her feet coated in sand. She could hear the spit and crackle of fires burning: a drum beat tapped by hands on a soft leather hide, the heat was close. Helen stood firm. Before her were five funeral pyres. They were all burning, except for the one in the centre. Around them the fire-stokers, oiled and half naked, poked at the fires. Another man rushed past, dousing her with funeral ash, then another did the same. Both vanished when she looked at them.

The silver-grey dust settled on her wet skin and covered her face. In the shadows she heard Nana: 'Free yourself… free yourself.'

She approached the pyres and found between the raging fires a man, still living, bound to the funeral pyre. It was Jack. His mouth silenced by a cloth, he looked at her, his eyes begged her. Standing before him was the girl from the temple: the child in the room, bathed in the ashes of the dead.

Nana held out a burning flame. 'Free yourself.'

She took it. Jack struggled under the stacks of wood, unable to break free. As Helen passed the flame over his face, he felt its fury. She lit the fire. The pyre erupted as Agatha's words echoed in her ears: *David was your father. David.*

FIFTY

Sunrise

Across the Varuna, settled beneath the trees, Kasi swigged some water from his canteen. Lying on his back, he looked up through the dappled light breaking through the tree branches. He took another sip and rubbed his eyes. He'd spent the night in the forest. On his front, lying low behind the shrubs, he kept watch through the viewfinder of his camera.

The forest was alive with birdsong. Helen was asleep, lying on her side. The rising sun burned out the morning sky, as rays of warm sunlight brushed her skin, waking her. And when she woke, what she saw took her by surprise. The fire had been stoked, and two fish impaled on sticks were cooking on it.

A passing breeze tingled her bare skin. Her clothes hung off a line tied from the tree to the shack: her vest and bottoms, still dripping, were draped to dry. She found that she was wrapped in a translucent white saree from breast to thigh. She stood up and felt the clothes – they were still wet. Beyond the tree, she found Nana in the river. She felt different; not afraid.

The pendant resting under her throat felt less heavy. Her mind was rested, and her body and spirit felt strong: she felt as though she had defeated a terrible fever and awoken cleansed and guilt-free. She tried to remember the night before – walking through the forest and arriving at the shack. The rest remained a dreamy blur that made little sense.

Kasi leaned forward in the dirt. His focus shifted to Helen as she appeared on the bank. He snapped and snapped, increasing the zoom as the sunlight filtered through her saree, exposing her figure beneath it. The pendant filled the frame.

'Tulsi,' Kasi whispered.

'What happened last night?' Helen asked Nana.

Nana, basking in the sun's rays, his eyes closed, replied, 'You freed yourself from your pain.'

'My clothes?' She felt uneasy about asking.

'You fainted and stumbled into the river. I changed you. Don't let that trouble you – after all, we are just flesh and bone. It's what's inside that matters: your soul.'

Anyone else would have been troubled by a stranger seeing them passed out, cold and naked. It should have bothered her, but she chose to ignore it. Something more had happened, beyond her modesty: she had changed inside.

'I saw things,' she said, unable to express any recollections with clarity.

But Nana had shared her dream, and he led her through it – he knew what she saw, and the girl in the temple was gone. He expressed it as best he could.

'The reason for your pain... he's gone now,' said Nana as he vanished beneath the water. When he came up, he was facing her. She was standing, her saree shining brightly in the sun. She appeared purified and freed by the holy water, by a goddess, by Ganga – that's what Nana believed.

It hit her. 'Jack.'

Nana looked right at her. 'Jack... he's gone.'

She recalled the pyres.

Nana walked out onto the bank, unclothed and dripping. Helen turned away. He had no shame about exposing his body.

'Why do you shy away from seeing me? You don't shy away from a stray dog or bird in the sky. They are as the maker created them, so I am as the maker made me.'

Helen took her clothes off the line and rinsed as much water from them as she could, and put them on. By the time Nana appeared, she was ready to leave.

'For you I have covered up,' he teased her. Nana pulled out the fish, which were cooked to perfection. He passed her one, on a stick, as he took a bite of his.

'I don't know what you did last night, but whatever you did, I'm grateful.'

'Don't be. Whatever you feel happened was of your making, not mine.'

Kasi slid backwards into the trees. He'd seen enough. Perched behind a tree, he flicked through the photos in the camera screen. There was one that brought a smug smile to his face. He increased the zoom to max. The silver vines branching across the pendant were the reason for his glee. He leaned back against the tree, confident that his journey was coming to an end.

FIFTY-ONE

After an uncomfortable night, Rajveer ached all over. Her neck was stiff from leaning against the jeep's hard doorframe all night.

'Chai?' A boy knocked on the door. He'd brought her tea, just as she'd ordered the tea vendor the night before, leaving him instructions to wake her if she hadn't woken herself by 7.30 a.m. Trapped in a deep sleep, she shook, as the knock's got louder.

She took the tea and picked up her mobile. The battery was dead. She could see the hotel entrance behind her in the rear-view mirror.

'Shit,' she said, and grudgingly went inside.

The manager had been replaced by an equally displeasing receptionist, who was busy chatting to a busy working girl, his fingers playing with hers over the desk as they whispered secrets to one another like adolescent teenagers.

Rajveer broke in, tapping her police baton on the desk. At first he ignored it, but as she persisted he turned to her. She wasn't going to put up with his chatter. She spotted some messages pinned to a tattered chipboard. One had her name marked on it, along with a college name: *ALLAHBAD WOMENS COLLEGE – SAVITRI JOSHI*. It was from Arjun.

The college was located on the other side of the city. The early morning grind of traffic laced the highway with choking diesel fumes, making it difficult to breathe. By 9 a.m., however, Rajveer had arrived on a busy street and asked a passer-by for directions. He pointed to a flat-roofed mid-terrace building, five storeys high, labelled with a dozen different hoardings scattered across the walls and between the window frames. Peering through the jeep's window she scrutinised each floor and finally found a hand-painted sign for the college on the fourth floor.

Arriving at reception she flashed her badge. The receptionist called for the manager. While waiting for him, Rajveer strolled through the lobby. The college was made up of five classrooms, cramped and full of female students of varying ages. As well as the reception desk, there was a small reading room and a narrow space between two rooms where a teenager was cooking food for the staff and students. The posters stuck to the walls offered basic English courses and a small selection of secretarial and typing classes. Under the college's logo, it boasted of its affiliation to the Oxford University of Women's Studies. On paper, it gave the college a superiority well beyond the realities of its true operations: apart from a glossy website and contact submission page, absent of phone numbers, it was a harmless illusion that helped the owners draw in fee-paying students.

'Excuse me,' the manager said. He was a trim, tall man, with the polish of a salesman. 'Anything wrong?' He picked up on Rajveer's interest in the Oxford connection. It didn't escape him that a few weeks back the authorities had closed down a college claiming false connections to another famous university in England.

'Are you the manager?'

'Yes, I'm Mr Akram. Is there anything I can do for you?' he said, wondering how much it was going to cost him to pay her off.

'Oxford... England... really?' She played with him, taunting him. She needed to access his records, and wondered how best to play it.

'So, I need to see your student records. Where are they?'

'Sorry?'

'Your records.' Rajveer walked in front of him, leading him to his office, and pointed to his computer. Mr Akram sat down. Following her instructions, he typed in Savitri's full name and searched the database. Her name appeared along with the course she had undertaken: Advanced Typing and English. She'd received a pass on both. The 'fees paid' column showed her fees paid as zero. Her address in the city was also missing, and there was no contact number either. It didn't give Rajveer much to work with.

'Is that it? What about her contact details?'

He just shrugged. The truth was, Savitri had paid her fees in full, in advance and in cash – on condition she didn't have to give any contact or address details. Rajveer figured the same.

'What can you tell me about her?'

'Nothing. I just run the place – we have hundreds of students come and go each year.'

'But this one paid in cash, didn't she?' Rajveer pointed to the zero in the paid column, where those above and below all had various fees marked in. 'Well? I could arrange for a thorough check on all your fee records. Taking cash and not declaring it – do you know how much trouble you're in? Well...'

'Mr Ayub – speak to him.' He got up and led her out to the classroom at the end of the lobby, and barged in. Mr Ayub stopped his English class. The students looked at Mr Ayub with suspicion. What did the police want with him? He wondered the same. Outside the class Mr Ayub was introduced to Rajveer as Savitri's English teacher. She asked him if he recalled anything about her, and he did. She was a bright student, a fast learner, having been taught out of college hours by Kasi. Mr Ayub recalled her close friend, Sunita Rao – they had studied the same course and often arrived and left together. He didn't recall Kasi or any other man coming with either of them. They went back to the computer and found Sunita's record, along with her address. She lived close by, in an apartment complex south of the main railway station.

Much to relief of Mr Akram, Rajveer left with the address in her hand. Fighting her way through the city traffic, she got as far as she could before she decided to walk the remaining distance by foot. It wasn't far, but the traffic was gridlocked. She walked through the old city with its bustling markets with spices and rags, then along a side alley where she asked a local spice vendor for directions. She was close: the vendor flipped his hand left to right and left again and indicated up to a higher floor.

Behind the chaos of the main bazaar, where the noise settled down to a polite exchange of chat, on the second floor of a green-painted building, which had endless balconies full of drying clothes, Rajveer arrived at Sunita Rao's apartment. She pulled back the security grille and entered the hallway, then knocked on the middle door, but no one answered. She peeked through a coin-sized hole in the wooden window board, but there was nobody inside. Noting the time, she leaned over the balcony and looked around at the kids playing cricket in the alley below. A door opened behind her. It was a neighbour, coming to see what the police wanted.

The middle-aged woman confirmed her neighbour was Sunita Rao, and she was far from pleased with her antics. 'She comes and goes as she pleases, late in the night, sometimes in the early morning – it's not right,' she said, unable to bring herself to spell it out: that Sunita worked as a prostitute.

FIFTY-TWO

With a purposeful stride, Helen crossed the courtyard just as Arjun was enquiring about her whereabouts of Agatha, who appeared visibly upset by her absence. They saw her just as she saw them. Regardless, she headed to her room.

'Helen... Helen,' said Agatha, but her call was ignored. 'Look, she's back now, that's all that matters. I'll speak to her.' Agatha left it to Arjun. She'd confided in him when he arrived to follow up with Helen about her day in the market with Maya, but Helen was still missing from the night before. Agatha was worried sick. Sarah's suicide haunted her. She had terrible thoughts that Helen might do the same as Sarah had done, unable to cope; that she might end it all.

Helen washed her face and dried herself with a towel, still glowing from the night's spiritual relief. She changed her clothes and sat on the bed, looking around the room, wondering whether to stay or go. She picked up her bag, opened it, and pulled out the leather-cased photo album and flicked through it. There were photos of her with Sarah, as a baby, as a child, and together as mother and daughter on the beach in Brighton. There were none of Jack. She finally came across one of Sarah, a black-and-white photo, taken when she was ten. Besides her was Agatha, also ten. Helen's eyes filled with tears as she touched the photo.

'Helen, it's Arjun. Can I come in?'

Helen closed the album and wiped her tears. 'Just a minute.' She picked up the towel and washed her face once more to conceal the tear stains.

'Come in.'

'Hey, how are you?' he asked.

'Why? What did Agatha tell you?'

'Nothing. She's just worried. I'm not here to pry, but she's a good lady, she really is, so whatever has happened between you two, I hope you can work through it, for the sake of you both, and for this place. She's the rock. Without her... you understand, right?'

'I appreciate it. I take it you're here about Maya? I've been over that day again and again, and... nothing unusual stood out. I'm sorry.'

Arjun glanced around the room at the table and wooden shelf. Apart from some books and folded clothes, the room was bare. He noticed a stack of photos on top of a guidebook, and asked permission to look through them. The photos were those Helen had bought from the photographer in the ghats. As well as being good, the framing stood out: they didn't look like casual snaps but rather were carefully composed. Someone had taken their time over them, waiting for the right shot before taking them.

'These were taken on the same day?' he asked.

'Yes, they were. The guy kept bugging us about buying them... Maya tried to stop me, but I gave up in the end and bought them. But the guy was harmless. I didn't think much of it. He just seemed too busy snapping photos of anyone, looking for a quick buck.'

'Strange – these don't look like they've been taken by someone in a hurry.' He shuffled through the photos.

'Can you describe him to me?'

'Just a young man with a camera – he had a cap on, a baseball cap, he was thin and spoke pretty good English, and was full of himself, if you know what I mean.'

Bothered by the quality of the photos, Arjun decided to follow it up. He asked Helen to come down to the ghats with him to see if she could identify the photographer. Agatha watched them as they left. She didn't interrupt, content to see her back safe. The rest could wait for later.

FIFTY-THREE

Tourist touts and local snappers gathered on the riverbank, close to Scindia Ghat where the photographer took photos of Maya and Helen. Behind a chequered wooden grille, Helen watched, with Arjun by her side. A dozen young men, all locals, had been rounded up and huddled into a single file, front-facing to form an identity parade so that Helen could get a clear view of each of them as they were rotated one by one.

Above the steps, overlooking the ghats, from the privacy of a terrace balcony, Kasi watched with caution. The police's interest in the photographers meant only one thing: they were closing in on him. He decided to retreat from the old city and prepare for this final act.

Down below, Helen watched as the second rotation of the same men sped through, but the photographer they had seen was not among them. By now a crowd had gathered, uneasy with the police's manhandling of their friends and relatives so harshly in public, and the photographers became agitated and vocal.

Arjun passed Helen his binoculars. 'Please take a closer look. Are you sure he's not one of them?' But she was. A tourist boat docked nearby. A handful of tourists strayed onto the rising steps, and among them Helen noticed the baseball cap.

'Wait...' She looked through the binoculars. 'Yes... that's him, the one with the cap.' She pointed towards him. Arjun looked through and saw him too.

'Are you sure?' he asked. She was.

'There's a guy with a baseball cap coming up the steps – bring him to me,' he commanded the lead officer on his two-way radio.

The rest of the photographers were escorted away so that their details could be taken down. Another three officers moved in on the man with the cap, who caught on to the officers' approach. He and his friends tried to change direction, but the officers nabbed him and pinned him down.

'Are we done?' Helen asked, keen to leave.

'For now. If we need you, I'll send for you.' Arjun ordered an officer to drop her back to the mission.

On the steps in front of Arjun, following a quick search, the officers picked up the man and led him to Arjun, who was waiting inside the covered dome. The man was terrified and held on either side by officers. His head drooped, his posture was submissive, he didn't put up any fight – but that didn't rule him out from being the killer.

'What's your name?' Arjun asked.

'Sir, I've done nothing wrong, you must be…' But before he had finished, an officer clipped him on the back of his head, flipping his cap off, adding, 'Sir asked you your name.'

The man stuttered. 'Sir, Vishal… Vishal Singh.'

Arjun took his camera and pouch. Running through the digital photos and printed copies, he asked him, 'You're from where?'

Vishal answered, 'Mirzapur, sir, Mirzapur.' It was a town fifty kilometres south-east of Varanasi. 'Sir, if you tell me what you're looking for I can help.'

The digital photo card contained several dozen photographs, but none of them were from the day Helen and Maya spent in the market. Vishal had already wiped his card to free up memory space to take new photographs.

Vishal pleaded with the officers that he'd done nothing wrong as Arjun compared his photos with the ones he'd taken from Helen. There was a clear difference: Vishal's shots were hurried, unlike Helen and Maya's composed ones. Arjun showed Vishal Helen's photos.

'You took these, didn't you?'

Vishal recognised Helen and Maya. 'No, sir, they are not mine.'

'I have an eye witness who says you took them.'

'They are not mine, I....' He went on to confess he'd taken them from a bin. The locals shared a printing machine inside a local store. When Vishal had gone there to print off his own photos, he had found these, discarded in the bin. He knew they were taken by Kasi – the quality was superior to his – and he took them to try his luck at selling them. Having hard copies to hand always made a difference when sealing a deal with tourists.

Arjun pressed him. 'If they're not yours, then whose are they? You know whose they are, don't you!'

'Sir, his name's Kasi... Kasi, he takes photos like me.'

'Kasi... where can I find him?'

'Sir, I've not seen him for a few days. He comes and goes, keeps to himself. I can show you where he stays; it's not far from here.'

Vishal was cuffed and escorted to the police jeep, and his camera confiscated. As they passed through the alleys, the locals speculated on the reasons for the police presence. Vishal kept his head down, weeping, afraid the police would beat him in custody if they found nothing at Kasi's place. The jeeps left and headed down the back road towards Assi.

FIFTY-FOUR

Late Afternoon

Red and green light painted the room inside Sunita's neighbour's apartment, filtered through the tinted window. Rajveer finished off a packet of barley biscuits as the neighbour replenished her tea – her third. She'd spent the past hour hostage to the neighbour's whining: frustrations built up over a number of years, vented in a single serving.

Sunita did work as a prostitute, or an escort, visiting cheap hotel rooms to pleasure anyone willing to pay: well-off students, unhappy middle-class husbands, and travelling businessmen – all sorts.

She first befriended Savitri at college, when they had both seemed like outsiders, lacking in confidence: her, the secret working girl and Savitri, the Dalit from Banaras – they were bound to be drawn to one another. The course was meant to help her attain a better life, but she had become accustomed to the money she made as a prostitute – anything from 3,000 to 4,000 rupees a night, and sometimes double, especially when the client was a businessman from out of town, marooned inside a five-star hotel, desperate for company.

The money was far more than she could make in an administrative job. It got her a small apartment in a respected residential street, with clusters of self-regulating middle-class do-gooders who sheltered from the realities of the world outside their gated compounds. She felt equal, so she didn't care how she made her money. And quite apart from the money, she enjoyed it – business and pleasure, that's what made her customers come back time after time, because with her, most of the time it was for real.

She'd stopped working for a while as her friendship blossomed with Savitri, but she never escaped the life completely and after Savitri returned to Varanasi, like an addict it wasn't long before Sunita fell back into the work.

Rajveer checked her watch. The dial had barely moved since the last time she had checked, three minutes earlier. Then a padlock rattled outside the open door and the neighbour standing in the doorway grunted as she saw Sunita arrive home.

Hastily Rajveer said goodbye to the neighbour and left her apartment. Outside was a woman, tall and slim with a disproportionately large bust. She was wearing a cocktail dress well before the usual cocktail hour, and holding a designer purse. She bore the remains of a lipstick kiss between her ear and neck; she'd forgotten to wipe it off.

'Sunita Rao?' Rajveer asked her.

Rajveer flashed her police identification badge and gestured for Sunita to go inside. Sunita, accustomed to dealing with the police, paying them off in cash or sex – male or female, she'd done it all – even dared to inspect the badge, noticing that she was from Varanasi.

'You're a long way from home,' she teased. 'Looking for company? Let me guess, Priya sent you.' She speculated an introduction from a regular female officer she kept company with.

'Inside, now!' Rajveer was in no mood to play. She stepped in and invaded Sunita's space, rummaging through her clothes on the rack – she had foreign brands of jeans and tops, and expensive make-up on the table.

'Look, you can't just come in like that.'

'Sit down,' Rajveer commanded. Sunita sat.

'What's she been saying?' she asked, referring to her neighbour.

'Savitri Joshi.'

Sunita stopped dead.

'Good friends, weren't you? Studied at the same college… did she live here?'

'No, she—'

'She was also a call girl,' Rajveer cut in.

'No, don't say that, she was never that. She was... a friend.'

'A friend, a good friend? Then you knew her well.'

Rajveer looked through the books in the shelf.

'Then you must have met her boyfriend?'

'Kasi? Yes, I did. The three of us hung out together, but after she left I never heard from her again... not until... I received a letter from Kasi after her death. He was the one who told me about how she... died.'

'This Kasi – are you still in touch?'

'No, not for a while. The letter was the last time I heard from him. Is he in any trouble?'

'What about a contact number, address for him?'

Sunita had nothing to say. She was growing anxious. Why had a police officer from Varanasi tracked her down?

'This Kasi, was he at the same college?'

Again Sunita had nothing to offer.

'And Savitri – any idea why she changed her surname to Joshi?'

'That was Kasi's surname – Kasi Joshi.'

Sunita asked permission to get up, then pulled out a tattered suitcase from under her bed and brushed off the dust. She went through some paperwork inside it, and came across her course certificate and some photos, among them one of her with Savitri, and another one that included Kasi, hugging Savitri to him. Sunita passed it over.

'That's all I have.'

Rajveer, holding the photo, was fired up. She was relieved to have found a significant lead – something Arjun had not. A part of her, the competitive side, salivated over the find. The other side of her knew she had to get back to Varanasi and call it in. She asked for her phone and dialled Arjun. His phone rang out. She left a brief message, and snapping a photo of Kasi using her phone's camera, she sent it to his mobile. She redialed her team's phone, but again no one answered.

'Can I ask... am I in trouble?' Sunita asked.

'No,' said Rajveer, then left.

FIFTY-FIVE

The police jeeps trailed in one after the other along a back road, a hundred metres from the old mill building. Inside, Vishal gave them directions. Along with several armed officers, they spread out in both directions, spreading around the building to ensure every exit was covered. Eventually the remaining officers, along with Arjun, came to the grilled gate, and entered. A family lived in the grounds of the mill, and Arjun asked them for Kasi. He was pointed to the upper floors. Officers quietly escorted them out as the second team made their way up the uneven staircase.

They came to the landing, which was littered with brick rubble and broken glass, with a single door at the end. They passed through it, cracking the shards of clay, making a noise that would alert others to their presence. Arjun fired two shots at the lock, then paused. There was no response. They kicked in the door.

Arjun peered inside, but there was no sign of Kasi. He kept the officers outside as he observed. The first thing he saw was the framed photo of Savitri with a Tulsi garland He broke a leaf off it: it was still crisp and scented. There were photos hanging by a thread, imprinted on the back with today's date. A plastic container caught his eye – the cap off, it reeked of petrol. A camera dangled from its strap from a rusty nail pinned into the wall. There was no doubt left: Kasi was the man they were looking for.

The officers melted behind the doors and terraces, keeping out of sight. All Arjun could do was sit and wait for Kasi to return.

FIFTY-SIX

Sunset

The fisherman steadied his boat as his young son dropped anchor. When the boat was still, the fisherman swung his fishing net out and quietly waited for the fish. Downstream, under the gentle current of the river, Kasi escaped the world above. The deathly silence consoled his tortured heart as he prayed for release from his life. His eyes opened and, when he rose from the water, he was calm. Staring up at the sky, his hands raised to the sun, he whispered, *'Moksha, Baba… moksha.'*

A flaming ray cut through the ripples in the river as sunset fell. Nana brushed his fingertip over Kasi's forehead, marking him with a bright red tilaka, a holy blessing. Beaming with pride, he looked at Kasi like a father bidding farewell to his son on the eve of a great battle, knowing it would be the last he would see of him. Kasi was a perfect student, and had never questioned Nana – until now, that is. He believed in Nana, every word he said, but for the first time, as his journey was coming to an end, he was confronted with doubts. A sense of guilt crept in as Kasi prepared to meet his maker. Nana saw it in Kasi's eyes, and took his hands.

Two years earlier

Nana was the one who had found Kasi, beaten and left for dead. Kasi, his eyes blurred with blood, barely breathing, was pulled from the river by Nana. During the night Nana lit a fire inside a cave by the river. Nana waited, watching Kasi whine in pain, and when he could scream no more, he called out one name over and over: 'Savitri… Savitri'. Nana heard it through the night. A part of him saw nothing more than a dying man who would soon cease to be. Another part of him, the part that drove him to save Kasi from death, questioned whether fate was playing its hand: a test in the form of a living soul that he, and only he, could decide whether to aid him, or abandon him to die. Looking at him, curled up like a frightened creature, Nana could have granted him mercy and let him die, but instead he decided to prolong Kasi's pain. The gods had delivered Kasi, and Nana left it to the gods to determine his fate. If Kasi made it through till first light, only then would he help him.

As dawn broke, Nana reached over Kasi and wiped his forehead with water. He was alive. Over the coming days Nana tended to Kasi's wounds, and the blood dried and his wounds scabbed over as his strength slowly returned. In that time the two formed a mutual bond as student and master. Nana had finally found a worthy pupil and Kasi a complex character that his lens could never capture. As the days passed, Kasi fell further into Nana's world, layer by layer: in his mind, material things became worthless and his bond with Savitri was slowly breaking. This only changed when he learned she'd taken her own life. Then rage filled his belly and he demanded that his master help him.

Sunset – present

'You promised me, Baba, that you would reunite me with Savitri,' said Kasi.

'And I will… in death. You have faith in me, don't you?' Nana felt Kasi's hands tremble.

'It was I who brought you back from the dead, I who gave you life.' Nana held Kasi's right hand and rested it on his beating chest. His heart thumped through the cloth.

'That night, when you walked around the sacred fire seven times, you made a pact with Savitri, a bond that no mortal can break.' Kasi felt the beat of Nana's heart.

'Then show me, Baba, show me your power – give me back my Savitri.' As Kasi begged, he felt a change in Nana's pulse. It slowed down noticeably. He looked into Nana's eyes, and again his pulse slowed – then vanished completely. Kasi moved his hand and pressed hard against Nana's skin, but his pulse had gone. It was a yogic breathing technique Nana had learned, so advanced that very few had managed to perfect it. To stop one's heart for a few moments, long enough for others to believe he was dead. Kasi looked at Nana, in awe of him, his master.

FIFTY-SEVEN

The sky turned a darkish blue as the ghostly imprint of the moon appeared. The highway sign read *85km to Varanasi*. The jeep was jerking as steam fizzed beneath the bonnet. Rajveer pushed the pedal to keep up the pace, changing gear to thrust forward, but the jeep's power was fading. A loud clunking sound finally halted the jeep, and a gush of steam broke out from under the bonnet. The engine was knackered. Rajeeer pulled off the highway and opened the bonnet. The engine was coated in oil and she had no idea what to do about it; she was no mechanic.

Rajveer stepped onto the highway and signalled for a lift, but the traffic, was little there was, sped past. A truck appeared, still some distance away, and she moved into the middle of the road to flag it down. As it approached, she signalled it to halt, holding out her police ID. The driver kept going, sure the obstructor would step away, but she didn't, and as he neared he realised she was a police officer. He slammed on the brakes, making dust billow out from under the wheels, and the truck came to a stop. Rajveer walked around to the driver's side.

'Varanasi.' She held up her ID to his window. He was heading that way. He leaned over, brushed the remains of his lunch off the passenger seat, and let her in from the other side.

FIFTY-EIGHT

Sunset

After returning from the ghats, Helen spent the rest of the afternoon gathering her thoughts. Part of her was desperate to get away and return to London. What kept her from leaving was the thought of the scars she would return with, knowing that Agatha, not Sarah, was her birth mother. She had so many questions to ask.

Agatha prayed in front of the wooden cross, and a few candles flickered in the darkness, bronzing the Christ's wooden skin. She begged for forgiveness.

'I should never have left her.' She wept in remorse.

'I abandoned her, my own child… I abandoned her.' Her head sank in shame.

Helen waited outside; she heard everything. And when she'd heard enough, she came inside and sat by her mother's side. The two embraced as mother and daughter, holding one another as they both cried.

Night

There was no sign of Kasi, as Arjun ripped the top of a second pack of cigarettes. He lit one and sank back onto the bench. With a quick flick of his wrist, he checked the time: a few minutes past ten. He put an order in for another shot of tea.

Inside the yard, between the old mill building and an adjoining building, an officer watching from above heard tin cans being kicked in the alley. It was too dark to make anyone out, but someone was coming. The officer called it in and quietly Arjun strolled inside. He was met by three other officers. Armed, they approached the mouth of the alley's narrow opening. From above, the officer on the roof terrace took aim.

At first sight of the man, the officers bundled him to the ground and muffled his head with a rag cloth until he was cuffed. They turned him over. Seeing the guns, he was stunned silent. Multiple torch rays flashed across his face, and the police saw he was nothing more than a homeless drunkard. The officers escorted him out the same way he had come in. Arjun returned to the tea stall and took his seat at the bench. In his mind, there were only two outcomes to the night: either Kasi would return and he would catch him, or he wouldn't and they'd have to expand their search in the morning. He hoped for his own sake it wasn't the latter. He feared Kasi's no-show meant he'd been tipped off. Still he waited, merging back into the crowd of Assi's tea drinkers.

FIFTY-NINE

On the other side of the old city, barely four kilometres east of Assi, Kasi emerged from the shadows. He was carrying his bag along with a foot-long metal bar. Along an empty lane, he found what he was looking for: a parked rickshaw. Inside, the driver was asleep. Kasi waited across the lane until no one was in sight. He approached the rickshaw, firmly holding the metal bar. Through the window he saw the driver was sleeping, his head pillowed on a folded blanket. Kasi launched in and smashed the bar down on the driver's head. His head split open. Kasi struck him again, just to be sure, then pulled the man's body out of thee rickshaw and left him in the gutter. He rummaged through the man's pockets until he found his identity card. He took it and left in the rickshaw. The body was bound to be found, but Kasi didn't care; he had other plans. He took off and made his way through the city, stopping for no one as would-be passengers hailed him.

Inside the market Helen was finished. She'd spent her money and gathered her bags. She'd purchased a few gifts for the children – colouring pens for the boys and bright bangles for the girls. Exhausted, she took refuge at a street stall, where she ordered some snacks and a chai. Through the front window of a rickshaw, however, she was being watched. Barely thirty metres away, the driver lit up a cigarette as he waited for her. A passer-by tried to get in the back seat, instructing the driver to take him to his hotel, but the driver shooed him off; he wasn't interested. The passer-by got out, unhappy as his hotel was far away and there were no other rickshaws around. After exchanging a few insults, he walked away, but the driver stayed, watching Helen as she finished her tea and settled her bill.

Then the driver started his engine and turned on his lights. He pulled up next to Helen as she came out.

'Rickshaw, mam?' he asked politely. She gave him the address and he agreed to take her. As he made his way out of the market, the passer-by he had refused to take saw

Helen in the rickshaw. He yelled abuse at him, frustrated that he'd taken her instead of him. The driver ignored him and moved on. The ride was a touch faster than Helen had experienced before, but the lanes were largely empty so he made good speed.

'It's OK to go a bit slower, please.'

The driver dropped his speed as he made his way through the maze of poorly lit back lanes.

At the same time, outside the police station, the truck driver stopped beside a line of empty rickshaws. Rajveer thanked him, got out and made her way into the police station. Unusually, she found the reception area empty. Outside, the police jeeps were also gone. An officer came down the stairs.

'Where is everyone?' she asked him.

'At Assi Ghat, mam.'

'Why?'

'I don't know much, but I overheard one of the officers mention the serial killer had been tracked down, somewhere near Assi.'

Rajveer wasted no time and left, but without a jeep she found herself once again having to find a lift. Several vehicles approached her on the highway, but no one stopped. She looked inside the parked rickshaws to see if anyone was sleeping inside, but each one was empty, until she came across a driver curled up in the back of one. She poked him to wake him, and he moaned and woke. But he was drunk, his speech slurred, and she left him to it. Back on the highway a rickshaw finally approached her, with bright headlights. She covered her eyes. The driver stopped. Before he changed his mind, Rajveer jumped in the back.

'Assi Ghat,' she ordered, 'and make it quick.'

The driver did as he was told and sped down the highway.

Helen's driver continued down darker alleys. The turns got tighter as he navigated the cobbled paths that were more suited for walking than rickshaws, and his side mirrors grazed against the bricks as the path narrowed.

'Mam, you've been here long?' asked the driver.

'A few days,' said Helen. 'Is this the right way?'

'It's a shortcut, mam – you'll see,' the driver replied. He smiled at her as he caught her attention in the rear-view mirror. Helen sat back, occasionally looking out of the open sides of the rickshaw, catching a glimpse of a busy lane. The driver finally turned onto a wider lane, still empty of traffic and people, with only stray dogs and bullocks for company.

Blinding headlights caught Rajveer's driver by surprise. He slammed on the brakes to avoid colliding with a truck. The rickshaw wheels locked, forcing it to come to a screeching halt inches from the truck. The driver and Rajveer were thrown forward then back on their seats. Rajveer felt the sting of whiplash. The truck pulled around, and its headlights briefly lit up the inside of the rickshaw. In the rear-view mirror Rajveer found herself staring at the driver – it was Kasi. There was no doubt in her mind it was him; it was the same face from Savitri's graduation photographs. Her long stare left Kasi feeling the same. He accelerated, throwing Rajveer back, aggravating her whiplash. He steered off into the first alley before she could get out. He parked and beat her out, launching a volley of punches into her from the side; he didn't stop until she had been knocked out. His knuckles bruised and red, gasping for air, he stepped back. On the back seat Rajveer lay bleeding, a cut gouged across her brow from Kasi's ring. Kasi restarted the rickshaw and pulled away quietly.

A short time later, Helen's rickshaw arrived at the mission. The driver asked for a generous fee from his foreign passenger. He expected it and, having failed to agree a fixed price with him earlier, she had no choice but to pay him.

SIXTY

Arjun checked his watch again as the tea stall prepared to close up, the waiter taking last orders. Arjun ordered another glass of chai. As he waited for it, Kasi pulled into a builder's yard less than a hundred metres away. He turned off the rickshaw's engine and lights, parking it across the entrance to the yard. The yard was small, surrounded on all sides by residential houses. Many people had turned in for the night, so lights were off and blinds down. He had the privacy to go about his business in the heart of the old city.

He dragged the still-unconscious Rajveer by the arms. Her uniform was torn and soiled from the chipped rubble and masonry scattered across the ground. He finally leaned her against a cement pillar, and took out his bag. He used the rope and cloth from his bag to bind her, then adorned her neck with a fresh Tulsi chain and caressed her hair.

'It will be over soon for both of us,' he whispered.

Rajveer's eyes stung as Kasi poured petrol over her head. The stench choked her as it rained through her hair and bit at her wounds. The pain cut through her tied limbs. She cried out, but her cry was muffled by the cloth binding her mouth. She shook her head to wash out the petrol, but he kept pouring it. When Kasi was done, he walked behind her to the steps, lining the ground between Rajveer and himself with a pool of petrol.

Rajveer's eyes opened and closed several times until she found the courage to face him. Through a veil of blood, she caught a glimpse of his shadow, just in front of her, under a terrace, stacks of rusty scaffolding poles on either side of him. Kasi struck a match, and his eyes appeared out of the dark, seeming to glow like fire. She braced herself and forced her wrists against the rough grain of the rope, tearing her flesh.

Kasi watched her struggle as the match burned down. Its heat drew closer as it burned, but he waited for her to look at him one final time, and when she met him with a steely stare, no longer fearing his torture, he dropped the match into the pool of petrol.

The flame raced along the petrol trail he'd laid on the ground until it reached Rajveer, when it burst into life and torched her.

She screamed through the cloth as her hair singed and crisped. The fireball billowed as she tried desperately to break free. Kasi watched as she cooked in front of him. The walls of the yard were illuminated by the light from the fire, and her shadow jolted against the brickworks wall. Kasi screamed and cried out her pain.

'Savitri, Savitri!' he yelled. He picked up an iron bar and smashed it against a metal drum, beating and crying his loved one's name as Rajveer burned.

The cries awoke the ghat's residents. A woman appeared from the third-floor terrace across the yard and saw the flames. Another neighbour cried out of the window to fetch help. Kasi kept banging and shouting Savitri's name. A young man appeared and peered past the rickshaw at Kasi. He caught the madness in Kasi's eyes. Kasi was expecting someone else. The man ran down the cobbled path as more neighbours heard the noise and put their lights on, coming out to see what was happening.

The man appeared in the main street, shouting for help. 'Police, I need help! Police, please, there's someone on fire! Help, please!'

Arjun left his tea and went over to the crowd that was gathering around the man.

'Tell me what's happened.'

'A fire – someone's on fire,' the man cried out. He pointed down the dark alley, where, at its tip, they could see a faint glow. Arjun ran down the alley and another officer, who had been waiting behind Kasi's apartment block gate, followed.

Arjun could hear the fire rage as he saw the rickshaw ahead. The people above shouted to him as he came in sight of Kasi and the fire in the yard. Rajveer was still engulfed by flames. Arjun ran past the rickshaw and stood in front of the fire. There, on the ground, he found a broken name badge. It read *Rajveer Saxsena*.

Suddenly, the iron bar hit the ground and Kasi began to shout. 'She begged for mercy, she begged for her life, she begged and begged! Listen carefully – you can still hear her, begging.'

He came from behind the flames and stood in front of Arjun, who struggled to accept it was Rajveer tied to the post. Even though he held her name badge in his hand, it seemed impossible that the flaming body on the post was Rajveer.

'No, no!' Arjun said. He took off his shirt and pounded at the flames, but it was an impossible task. She was dead.

'It's her, your friend, your partner. I saw you together at the tea stall one night – what was her name? Her real name? Sunita Chandra Ram, yes… now you believe me?' Kasi taunted.

The hairs on Arjun's arms singed as he moved closer to the flames, but the heat from the fire defeated him; there was nothing more he could do. He stepped back and turned in rage, his hands clenched and eyes sharp. He was mild-mannered, but Kasi had unleashed the devil in Arjun. For the first time he wanted to kill someone, physically, with his bare hands, without mercy. Kasi hadn't shown any, and he deserved none.

'She's gone; there's only me and you left now,' said Kasi, his anger at last abated. As far as he was concerned, his work was completed. There was nothing more for him to do; he'd claimed his sacrifice. But there was something he needed Arjun to do.

'What are you waiting for? Let's finish this.'

Arjun stepped back and picked up the iron rod Kasi had dropped. Gripping it firmly, he stepped forward in Kasi's direction. Kasi paced towards Arjun, knife in hand. He cried out as he raised his right arm to charge: 'Savitri!'

BANG! The single shot from an officer's gun punched Kasi in the chest, and was followed by another shot to his heart, which dropped him to the ground. Kasi rolled in the chalky dust, his blood mixing with the white dirt. He leaned up on one elbow, choking on his blood as it filled his lungs. He said her name one last time then, smiling at the stars, he was dead.

The neighbours raced in with buckets of water, finally dousing the flames. What was left of Rajveer was unrecognisable; tarred in black. Her cooked flesh churned the stomachs of the onlookers, several of whom threw up. There was nothing anyone could do other than to show Rajveer dignity. Arjun tenderly wrapped his shirt over her head.

'Sir?' an officer called to him over Kasi's body.

Arjun knelt down by Kasi's side. His lifeless eyes gleamed in the moonlight.

'I've never seen that before,' said the officer.

'What?' Arjun asked.

'A dead man smiling,' replied the officer.

Arjun rolled his hand over Kasi's eyes and closed them.

SIXTY-ONE

A small army of police officers crowded around a freshly prepared funeral pyre. The corpse rested on neatly stacked logs. Much care had been taken to present the pyre, as a line of local photographers and journalists took turns to get their front-page photos. The more confident among them manoeuvred the police around to ensure the best-looking officers, lean, shaven and tall, were kept at the front. No expense had been spared; the best priest had been called in for the occasion. There were few mourners: apart from Rajveer's own team of officers, there was no family or friends. Arjun kept his distance. Mehra had made it clear to him earlier that his presence would not be welcome; Mehra held Arjun responsible for Rajveer's death – at least, that's what he wanted him to believe. The truth was more a convenience, Mehra's way of keeping the CBI out, leaving him to claim the glory.

He heeded Mehra's wishes, to a degree – he was not among them, but he was there, watching from the terraces overlooking the bank, away from the crowds and invited press. The journalist had a perfect story for their papers: tragic lovers, a brutal revenge, and best of all, a dead hero, Rajveer Saxsena.

Mehra tested the megaphone. 'Testing, one, two, three… testing, one, two, three.'

He'd drafted in the aid of a friend, Dilip Tiwari, who was an actor. This was his chance to build a platform for his political ambitions, and he wasn't going to let it slip by. Mehra gave the performance of a lifetime, addressing the crowd. 'She was the best of us, the bravest, never one to walk away. Rajveer Saxsena will be remembered for her courage, for her sacrifice. She is a shining example to all officers across Varanasi, across India, that we uphold the law without fear or prejudice, and in the face of death we shall not turn away.

'And to celebrate her life and her sacrifice, today I am proud to announce a special fund has been set up to help support a new generation of female police officers…'

Mehra's self-serving speech went on and on. It was far removed from who Rajveer Saxsena really was; the angry girl who ran away and changed her name from Sunita Chandra Ram.

The priest finished performing the last rites and, in the absence of any family members, he passed the bundle of flaming fire sticks to Mehra. As her superior officer, he was left to light the pyre. He placed it in the small opening. As smoke billowed through the stack, the shroud caught fire. It wasn't long before the fire came alive.

Arjun sat alone, praying for Sunita's soul – that's who she was, but it didn't matter any more.

It was over. He'd outlived his welcome in Varanasi, and it was time he moved on.

SIXTY-TWO

Five Days Later

The rusty old lock on the front door had been taken off and replaced with a shiny new one. Before Arjun closed the door, he strolled around the room one last time. He left a garland of fresh flowers in front of his parents' photo frame. He checked the window frame was sealed and, after one more glance, stepped out and sealed the lock. He passed by his neighbour's door.

'Arjun… come by from time to time: it's your home,' said his elderly neighbour.

'I will,' and he meant it. His bag in hand, he left, but before leaving he went to the police station one last time to say goodbye to Tripathi.

When he arrived, he found the office empty and the unit broken up, as officers found themselves reassigned to other cases. Arjun walked down the aisle to the back of the building and found Rajveer's desk had been cleared. Her plastic 1990s computer monitor was gone, along with her stacks of files and personal items. The room was bare, with only her desk and empty chair remaining. Arjun pulled out the desk drawer. Apart from a few paperclips and an empty notepad, it contained the photo frame he'd found when he first arrived. He took it and put it in his bag. The idea of leaving it there seemed wrong: they weren't his parents, but seeing them reminded him of his own parents, and he didn't want to see the frame end up in the rubbish bin, where it was most likely to go.

The phone rang on the outside office desk. He ignored it. The case was closed and his work was over: it was time to go home.

'Excuse me, sir,' said Tripathi, walking in. He had a file in his hand.

'Tripathi… I was about to leave. I just wanted to say goodbye.'

'I think you should see this.' Tripathi passed the file to Arjun. Inside he found a set of enlarged colour photos.

'We found four other digital cards at Kasi's place. These photos are printouts from them.'

'Helen…' Arjun ran through the photos. Several were of Helen wearing white cotton talking to Nana as he bathed in the river. Two were close-ups of Helen's Tulsi pendant.

'Tulsi?' He recognised the leaf design.

His attention then turned to Nana.

'Who's this guy?'

'I don't know, sir. I thought you might look into it.'

Arjun put his bag down and ran through the photos one more time. Over half were of Helen and Nana in the same location. It bothered him that Kasi had taken an interest in Helen's Tulsi pendant: the close-up was no mistake, as he'd taken several of them. And as for Nana, he wondered why Kasi had taken an interest in him as well.

He tapped the table with restless fingernails as his thoughts raced. The photos demanded answers.

'Come with me.' Along with Tripathi and the photos, he headed down to Mehra's office. There was no sign of him, but a passing officer remarked, 'If you're looking for sir, he's outside.'

The two hurried outside, and found Mehra about to get into his chauffeured car. Arjun stepped up to the car and held the door as Mehra sat inside.

'What is this… have you lost your mind?' He wasn't happy. He was already running late, and there was a sense of urgency in his tone. He had an interview to get to.

'Sorry, but sir...' Arjun held out the photographs. 'Please, this is important.'

'This better be good,' Mehra grunted. He flicked through the photos quickly, hardly glancing at any of them. 'What's this?' Before Arjun answered he continued, 'What have you got here? A foreign girl and a beggar in water?' He wasted no time in passing the photographs back.

'Sir, it's not so simple – Kasi took these pictures. This girl – she could have been a victim and—'

'And what? You think this means anything? Kasi's dead, Rajveer's dead – don't you think we've had enough now? We got the man, and my department paid a heavy price for it. Enough! Just go back to Delhi. The case is closed!' Mehra slammed the door shut, but before he took off he wound down the window and ordered Tripathi: 'Make sure you personally see him off to the airport. Make sure he catches his flight – is that clear?'

Tripathi had no choice but to nod in agreement. The window went up and the car took off, leaving Arjun angry. He slammed the file on a nearby bench.

'Arrogant bastard! Sorry.' But Arjun wasn't ready to let it go. 'I need a favour… but it'll probably get you into trouble.' He didn't need to plead much; Tripathi was in. Like Arjun, he didn't believe that the photos meant nothing.

'As far as he's concerned I'm gone – you saw me off.'

'Where will you be?' Tripathi asked.

'Around. I'll call you.' Arjun shook Tripathi's hand in gratitude and left, walking out through the gate and onto the main road. The chai vendor from across the road, who was outside fixing his broken sign, waved to him. Arjun waved back, recalling the conversation he had with Rajveer there.

A rickshaw pulled up beside him.

'Where to, sir?' the driver asked.

Morgue

The corridor echoed with the sound of chatter, and two porters pushed an empty trolley as they discussed a cricket match that was being held in Mumbai. The trolley wheels rattled and turned, then stopped. The door rolled back, and the suction released the chilled air from within. The porters lined up the trolley and pulled out Kasi's pale corpse, head first. His right foot was tagged with a label. One of the porters checked that the name on the tag matched the one on his clearance sheet. He ticked the box next to Kasi's name and marked the tag with a circle. Kasi's corpse was rolled down the alley and out through the doors.

SIXTY-THREE

Arjun dropped by the mission, looking for Helen, hoping she could shed light on the photographs. She was teaching at the orphanage. He made his way in and waited for her to finish. The children were quiet, attentive – they like her, Arjun thought, but she's not Maya. Helen saw Arjun standing at the back of the room and asked Bella to take over.

'I thought you'd be back in Delhi by now,' she said.

'Just tying up some loose ends. How are the children?'

'They miss her. I can't replace her – no one can.' They made their way to under a tree and sat down. Arjun pulled out the photographs from the river and passed them over to Helen, holding back the close-up photographs of the Tulsi pendant. Seeing herself half naked with Nana in the water made Helen uneasy.

'Who took these?' she asked. Arjun paused, before answering.

'They're from the camera of the guy who killed Maya.'

Helen flicked through them again, a little more slowly and with a worried look.

'He was following me? Was I a target?'

'I can't say, but there was nothing in his room that indicated you were.' He was lying; he didn't want to worry her any more than was necessary. She was visibly troubled. Apart from the photographs, he had nothing else, just an instinct. Kasi had sacrificed six girls and buried another. Arjun was plagued by the thought he was missing something. And why did Kasi wait around for the police? He could have run away, disappeared and killed again, but instead he waited – and was killed.

'Finish it,' echoed a voice in Arjun's head.

What did he mean by it? The officer wondered at Kasi's content face. There was more to it; Kasi's readiness to die still bothered him. For now, if someone else was involved he needed to give them room to play out any final act. But Helen could be at risk. He would need to strike before she was harmed. He needed her, as bait to prove his theory that Kasi was not a lone killer. There was someone else involved, and Arjun wanted to catch him.

So he kept calm and decided rather than increase her fears, he would tell her he was merely tying up loose ends before he left Varanasi.

'The pendant around your neck – can I take a look at it, please?'

Helen handed it over.

'It was my mother's. It's Tulsi,' she said.

'A symbol of an eternal bond,' Arjun finished with her. He passed it back to her, feigning unconcern rather than alarming her by telling her about its link to the murders.

'And this guy in the photo, where can I find him?' he asked.

'Nana? Why do you need to talk to him?' Helen became protective of Nana, anxious not to get him in any trouble. She wasn't sure how to explain their relationship and was worried about how he might be treated. A foreign girl, barely dressed in a thin saree with a local man – she worried they might blame him for something he didn't do. Drug abuse was rife, with foreigners flocking to Varanasi to smoke pot, and Nana would not be seen in a good light.

'Don't worry, it's just routine. He's in the photographs. If he wasn't, I wouldn't have to ask. And whatever is between you two is of no interest to me. I'm here to close the case. So please, this man Nana – where can I find him?'

Helen reluctantly pointed towards the riverbank. 'Go through that door, find the river bank and walk along it for about ten minutes or so. Once you get to a large tree overhanging the rise, if he's there, that's where you'll find him.'

Arjun wasted no time and left, forgetting to thank her. His mind shifted to Nana.

Deep inside the forest, where the light was dull, a funeral pyre waited to be ignited. Kasi's corpse rested on the branches, a white shroud covering his body so that only his face was visible. The rest of him was covered with more branches, and lumps of ghee filled the gaps, it helped fuel the fire. The birds seemed to sense the coming flames and in a single burst broke free from the treetops and escaped as Nana lit the pyre from below. He threw down the burning log and caressed his student's forehead one last time. He was not mourning his passing; he envied it. He placed a single Tulsi leaf inside Kasi's mouth. The fire leached its way up: first the smoke and then the flames pierced through the wooden branches. Nana rested besides a small fire as the pyre burned.

Meanwhile Arjun had arrived below the rise on the riverbank. He could see the large tree Helen had mentioned. He made his way up the muddy path and arrived on the plateau that overlooked the river below. There was little to see. Behind him was the forest. Arjun noticed the coloured threads tied around the tree stump a sign that someone priestly had stayed here, and the burned-out ash inside the rocks that had once held a fire He brushed his fingers through the ash; it was cold. A sound caught his attention – a snap of branches: it came from the forest behind him. Arjun stood up to take a look and crossed into the forest.

Nana sat quietly in a ray of sunlight that had broken through the trees. He remembered the last words Kasi had said to him: *I want you to have this. Open it when I am gone.* He had held Nana's hand in his and slipped an envelope to him. He knew what Kasi meant, and kept his word. He'd brought the envelope with him, and now pulled it from under his shawl. Nana broke the seal and emptied out the contents: money, some 30,000 rupees, made up of 1000-rupee notes, a letter and a folded photograph sealed with candle wax. Nana started with Kasi's letter. The paper flickered as he held it in front of the fire. Kasi's words seemed to come alive.

> *Remember the night you promised to unite me with Savitri for all eternity? You told me Savitri was damned for killing herself and that her eternal bond with me had been broken. Remember that night?*

You told me to believe in the power of God, that he is all that is good and evil, the creator and the destroyer, the fire and the wind. I believe you, Baba.

And I am proof of your power, which has brought a dead man back to life. I kept my promise to you: I gave you six souls as you asked. Now you must deliver the seventh, and last, soul to me.

You told me that the final sacrifice must be the greatest of all. You told me that I should be prepared to sacrifice the very things I longed to attain – moksha, Baba. I am asking you to honour your words and to sacrifice the thing you hold closest. She's been sent to us, Baba – she bears the mark of Tulsi.

Finish it, and unite me and Savitri for all eternity as you promised me, Baba.

Nana expected nothing less from Kasi; a gift that only a student could give his master. But he'd underestimated him. Then something unexpected happened. As Nana broke the wax from around the rim of the photograph and opened it out, her face appeared: it was a close-up photo, to avoid any doubt about who was to be the final, and greatest, sacrifice. The photograph was of Helen, and it had been taken by Kasi when Helen was with Maya in the old city.

Nana was lost for words. He was furious that Kasi had chosen Helen above all others. It was a deliberate choice; a test set by his student. He raged and crumpled the photograph in his fist and threw it into the fire.

'Kasi!' he cried out. He felt betrayed, taunted – his student, his disciple, dared to challenge him? As the photograph flamed, Nana kicked the fire with his bare feet and stood over the burning pyre. In the heat he could still make out Kasi's skull. The flesh was gone, Kasi was gone – his student was free. He let it go as he came to understand what Kasi had done. He wasn't testing Nana's resolve; he was reminding him of who he was. He was an Agahur – one who cared for no one, not even his student, his Kasi. So what was Helen, other than a passing distraction? No, she was more. Nana believed, like Kasi, she had been sent to Varanasi for a purpose – to form a bond with Tulsi, the Tulsi she carried around her neck: a bond that no man, no god could break. She was the one, the final sacrifice.

'I'll do it, Kasi. I'll finish it. I'll keep my promise.'

A branch snapped. Something – someone – was closing in. Nana turned around, grabbed his wooden staff from the grass, and stood ready.

'Nana, Nana?' Arjun called as he stepped further into the forest. Nana gripped his staff and raised it to strike, shielded behind a tree. Arjun stopped. He could see nobody. He decided to turn back.

Hidden behind the tree, Nana pulled out his staff and with both hands brought it down, cutting through the leaves and striking what turned out to be nothing more than a scavenging dog. It wasn't what he had expected. The dog stood no chance: its back broken, its pain was no match for the crackle of the burning pyre. Nana knelt down and held the staff across the dog's neck. He snapped it with a single blow, sparing it a slow and tortuous death.

Arjun returned to the dead fire and looked at the river once more. There was a fisherman, pulling his small fishing boat out of the water and onto the mud bank. Arjun went down to see him. The fisherman was busy tying how boat up when Arjun interrupted him.

'There's a priest who stays up there,' he said, pointing to the large tree perched on the plateau. The man kept busy with his work; he knew who Arjun was looking for.

'He's gone,' the fisherman replied, squeezing hard to form a tight knot.

'When?' asked Arjun, he joined the fisherman and pulled the rope tight.

'Thanks,' the fisherman said, appreciating the help. 'Yesterday.'

'Did he say where he was heading?'

The fisherman bunkered down with his catch of fish, which were still alive and fighting to escape inside a wooden barrel. He rested a wooden block between his legs and picked up a knife.

'No, that's his business. It's not the first time either. He comes and goes as he pleases – sometimes for a few days, sometimes for a month or more. But in the end he comes back. It's his home. Why?' The fisherman grabbed hold of a fish and laid it on the block, then cut its head off in a single movement. He then gutted the fish. The board stained with blood, he pulled out a second fish.

'The fish are getting smaller and smaller,' he remarked.

But Arjun had already left.

SIXTY-FOUR

The doors crashed open as the ambulance trolley pushed into them, and the two handlers continued their banter as they went from the ambulance into the morgue. Their loud voices quickly dropped as they found themselves among silent mourners – the joke they'd shared moments earlier had lost its humour. The receptionist demanded to see the paperwork. After briefly reviewing it, she stamped it, and the trolley proceeded from the reception room into the back corridors, where the two handlers continued where they'd left off, immune from emotion – they had to be, among the chilling corpses on either side.

A few minutes later Arjun came in, following a woman holding a child in her arms, aged no more than two. They were alone – her husband of three years slept, chilled in cold storage, on the other side of the doors. The widow's grief was stifled by the cold bureaucratic engagement she had to endure from the receptionist. The receptionist, although she was a graduate, lacked the charm to find a better job. She chewed gum as she pointed to the corner, where a bench lay in the darkness. She gestured again as the woman failed to follow her instruction, pointing more aggressively to the corner. Arjun stepped in and helped her to a better, well-lit seat currently occupied by a man, moving him to the darkness and keeping her firmly in the light.

'I need to see your records,' he said to the receptionist. After sizing him up and seeing his badge, she picked up the phone and called her manager, hidden away in the back office. He came through the door munching a bag of crisps, and wiped his hands on his shirt, brushing off the crisp crumbs. He inspected the badge himself.

'Is there a problem?'

'No, I'm just checking you have the correct authority,' the man replied. He took over from the receptionist, who used the opportunity to catch a smoke break outside.

The man turned to Arjun.

'Can I ask what you are looking for?'

'Kasi Joshi – his entry. He was brought here a few days back.'

'The one the police brought in?' He flicked through the pages, managing to read the records upside down until he found Kasi's name. He pointed to it. Beside the name there was a collection stamp.

'What's this?' Arjun asked.

'A collection stamp – the body was collected on…' he tapped the date under the stamp. It was today's date.

'Collected? You mean he's gone? Who gave the authority?'

The man called the receptionist back in. She took her time, puffing quickly at her cigarette before she had to throw it away. She was met with a quick fire of questions from Arjun: 'Who gave the release authority? Who took the body? What did he look like?'

The authority had come from Mehra's office, she said, after someone had arrived to collect it first thing in the morning. The receptionist, tired from a late night, had checked in with the police station. As the case was closed, the junior officer who answered the call found no reason to hold on to the corpse any longer, and authorised the release without checking further.

'The guy at the station said it was OK, so I released the body. I've done nothing wrong,' she said, unhappy at Arjun's inquisitive tone.

'What time?'

'I don't know, around 9 a.m. or so.'

'Where's the collector's name? There's no name here.' He pointed to the empty line under the collector's details. The girl looked at the stamp and empty line and then at her manager. There was no name – a lapse on her part – and she tried to defend it.

'He was in a hurry. As soon as the body was brought out, he led the porters outside to load it in the waiting farm truck, and he left straight after. There wasn't time to take his details.'

The manager stepped in. 'It happens. There's no harm done.'

Arjun pulled out Nana's photograph from his wallet and flicked it in front of the girl. 'Was this him?'

'Yes.'

'Are you sure?'

'I'm sure – you can't forget those eyes of his. I won't get into trouble, will I? I need this job.'

But Arjun had left, calling Tripathi as he walked back to the rickshaw. From inside he'd asked him to check in person all the burning sites along the ghats, to see if Kasi's corpse had been delivered for cremation.

SIXTY-FIVE

Old City, Afternoon

Slowed down by the pedestrian traffic, Arjun's rickshaw made slow progress through the old city and into the ghats. When the crowds became too heavy, he abandoned the rickshaw and made his way on foot through the narrow alleys on his way to the burning ghats. As he passed a line of local stalls he came upon a group of holy men. Lined up behind them was a small group of foreign pilgrims. The ashrams of Varanasi were filled with foreigners seeking spiritual awakening. It stirred him – perhaps Nana was a priest, and Helen was with him for spiritual guidance. Going back to ask Helen seemed a waste of time. Instead he decided to ask the local priests holding prayer sessions along the Ganges. There was an old priest among them, Arjun recalled, though he'd never spoken to him before, who would know whether or not Nana was a priest.

As Arjun arrived on the sandstone steps of Scindia Ghat, he saw the priest through the arches of the temple.

'*Jai Shiva Shankar*' – Praise be to Lord Shiva – the old grey-bearded priest said as he finished blessing a foreign woman who had travelled from Texas for her own spiritual awakening. Arjun waited to one side until she was finished. When she left, she was beaming with a sense of rebirth, a sensation not shared by Arjun, who until now, had never sought the company of priests.

'Come – sit down, my son,' said the priest, extending his hand in welcome. He was a smiley man, balding on top. Inside the stone temple, he watched over the Ganges, and inches from his feet, he had the best view of Varanasi.

Arjun flashed his CBI badge. As he did, he covered his printed name with his fingers. He didn't want his surname to end the conversation. He needn't have worried.

'Why did you cover your name?' the priest asked.

'I…' But before Arjun could answer, the priest interjected.

'A name is just a name – we are born with it, we die with it, but only God sees the life lived between it, not the name.'

'I wish there were more like you,' Arjun said. He pulled out the photos of Nana and Helen and directed the priest's attention to Nana.

'There's an old ruin in the forest beyond the Varuna River. This man Nana lived there. Is there anything you can tell me about him? Is he a priest of some kind?'

The priest pulled his glasses from under his clothes and put them on, then looked at the photos. There was a hint he knew Nana from his warm expression.

'Nana... a priest,' he said with affection. 'What do you want with him?'

'It's complicated. Where can I find him?'

'Well, not here, that's for sure. As you can tell from the photos, he prefers to keep himself on the outskirts, in the forests. Tell me, what do you know of the Aghori?' the priest asked.

'Aghori... those guys covered in ash? Nothing much.'

The priest went on to explain why Nana lived where he did, in the old cremation grounds. The cremation spot was small, barely visible from the forest and invisible from the river. But the stone markings around the site were not there by chance: small boulders had been sunk into the ground and marked by handprints dating back hundreds of years. One overlapped the other as the cremators passed from one generation to the next. But they, like Nana, were not related to one another in blood, but their bonds remained as strong, from Aghori to Aghori. Their secrets lived on.

'He's an Aghori,' proclaimed the priest, looking towards the river. There was respect in his words; a sense of envy.

'An Aghori? He doesn't look like one,' Arjun replied.

'Your eyes can deceive you. An Aghori in the truest sense is inward-looking and detached from everything. There are many who claim to follow this path. You can find them all around here, day or night, wandering around the burning ghats, bathing in the ashes of the dead – even drinking water from the skulls. It's quite a sight; such theatre.'

The priest favoured Arjun with a wide smile. He found the theatrics entertaining, useful antics for the visiting masses, giving the foreigners a sight to remember. But he was less jovial about Nana.

Inside the heart of a distant forest, Nana trailed his fingers through the heated white ashes of Kasi's remains. Nana absorbed the heat of the ash as he ground it between his palms. And when he was finished, he filled his hands with the ash and brushed it through his hair and down his face, changing his skin tone from light brown to silver grey. A thick coat formed around his body from head to toe: he was immersed in Kasi's remains.

Under the temple dome, the priest said to Arjun, 'To live as though you are a living god, free to do what you want, right or wrong, just to be. Tell me, could you do that in this city, along the burning ghats, where the eyes of so many watch over you?'

The priest pointed to the iron bridge in front of them, and beyond it the mouth of the Varuna River.

'The true Aghori lives out there, beyond the city, to do as he desires. Those that follow them do so blindly, doing whatever is asked of them.'

'Even killing?' asked Arjun.

The priest nodded. He passed the photos back to Arjun. As he left the temple and headed up the steps, he had the sense the priest was in awe of Nana – and he was right.

Making his way through the passages in the direction of the market, Arjun's phone rang. It was Tripathi with an update. He had nothing much to report – he had checked a string of cremation pyres but no one had accepted a corpse either by the name of Kasi or one delivered by Nana. They'd hit a dead end. Arjun was about to leave the passage, but a chance sighting of stacks of dry coloured powders caught his interest. He went up to the stall selling them: mini mounds of bright red, orange, green, blue and yellow powder.

Two college girls handed over a few rupees to the stall-holder, and in return he passed them ready-prepared pouches of various colours. The festival of Holi had arrived.

'When's Holi?' he asked the stall-holder.

'On Sunday, sir.' That was two days away. The stall-holder offered a bundle of pouches to Arjun.

'Sir, some Holi powder, sir, for the family, sir… sir.'

Arjun moved on, looking for a quiet place to gather his thoughts, which were spinning.

'Holi, Holi,' he muttered to himself, searching his mind, piecing together everything he knew about the case, the Tulsi, the brides, the victims' background. All fitted into place except one piece – Kasi.

He'd offered himself up, ready for death, and embraced it when it came.

'Why?' Arjun asked. 'Why?'

He had claimed six lives, not seven. His death had to mean more.

'He sacrificed himself,' shouted Arjun, stopping passers-by in their tracks. Then the final piece came to him. 'He gave up his life, so… so…. Nana, of course! The student, the master.'

It dawned on him, as the priest had said, that Kasi would have done anything Nana had said. And now Kasi was gone, Nana was free to strike – the case had been closed and police attention had moved on. And what better day than the day of sacrifice, Choti Holi, to light up a fire and complete the final act, the greatest sacrifice of them all – of Tulsi, of Helen?

Arjun called Tripathi to meet him at his father's place later, and ordered him to bring some items for him, they included some food rations and a gun.

SIXTY-SIX

He made one final wipe of the photo frames containing the photos of his mother and father, the shine so clear it sparkled. Fresh jasmine flowers scented the room, and everything was clean and in its place. Arjun oiled the latch on the window frame and, after a final look at the moonlit Ganges, he closed the window and sealed it. His bag rested on the bed. It was empty. The few clothes he'd brought with him were on the shelf.

'Sir?' Tripathi had arrived. He managed to take a quick look inside, and noticed everything was in place. It looked as if Arjun was about to leave, perhaps never to come back. Arjun greeted him at the door and, rather than bring him in, he sealed the door behind him, locking it with a new key he had had cut.

Tripathi kindly passed him the black sports bag Arjun had asked him to get.

Arjun opened it to check it.

'It's all there, as you asked,' Tripathi affirmed. 'Sir, if I may, perhaps I should at least come with you.'

'You've done enough, my friend. Any more and you'll risk losing your job, and I can't have that. Go home to your family. I'll call you if I need you.'

'Sir, but...'

'That's an order. Here, take this.' Arjun passed him the key. 'I've left some money behind the photo frames. I'd like it very much if you could look in from time to time, get the place cleaned up, and have some fresh flowers placed under my mother's photo. Jasmine, always jasmine. Can you do that for me?'

'I will. You're not coming back, are you, sir?'

'You're a good man – look after yourself.'

Tripathi watched Arjun walk out of sight and disappear into the alleys of the ghats. From there Arjun waited for a rickshaw – two came by, but neither driver was willing to take him out of the city. A third also refused, but this time Arjun used his authority to order the driver to take him. They left the quiet lanes of the old city as it drifted into silence, shutters all down and the footpaths cast only with the shadows of overhanging cables.

Several kilometres away, Agatha waded through her old photographs with Helen: a spread of photographs of Helen as a new born baby in Agatha's arms, of Sarah and Agatha as children, and another, which Helen held, of David and Agatha.

'Your father always wanted a girl; he picked your name – Helen, Helen of Troy, his beautiful daughter.'

'And if you had a boy instead?'

'He never doubted it – he just knew somehow you'd be a girl. He would have loved you so much.'

'And you didn't, so you gave me up and just left.'

'No. It was never like that. You were all I had of David. When I held you for the first time, I felt his heartbeat, and I never wanted to let you go.'

'But you did, and left me with a monster.'

'I never intended it that way. I just needed to get my head together. I was still mourning the loss of your father – my mind was awash with emotion. It was my mother's idea for me to take a few weeks out, to think things over. They wanted me to give you up for adoption, to be brought up with a mother and father. Your grandparents were old-fashioned. I don't blame them for what I did; it was a different time. So I left for a few weeks to think things over, and got as far away from home as I could. Varanasi was the perfect place, and once I arrived here, I knew I never wanted to go back. I sent Sarah a letter and asked her to look after you as her own child, and she did, and that was that. Life moved on and you had a secure home, a family.'

'But it never quite turned out the way you thought it would,' said Helen.

'Can I keep the letter?'

'Yes, of course,' replied Agatha. 'You're not planning to leave, are you?'

'I'm not sure I can stay much longer. Strangely, I miss the rain. I couldn't wait to leave home and now I know where I belong – and it's not here. I have a life to rebuild – my life, the way I want it. Just like you made this place your home, I'm sure I'll find my place in time.'

'The children have taken you to their hearts.'

'And so have I! They're amazing, every one of them. But my mind's made up – this is your home, not mine, and I need to find my own. It will take some time, but I'm sure I'll find it.'

'There's nothing I can do to change your mind, then.'

SIXTY-SEVEN

A dog, stretched out across the cobbles, found his sleep disturbed by the tremor of rickshaw wheels. He propped himself up on all fours and howled at it with annoyance, but it passed by without care. Arjun, chewing on his smoke, sat in the passenger seat and tapped the driver's shoulder to ask him to stop. He stepped out with his black bag and settled up with the driver. It cost him 150 rupees extra for the late-night drop-off at the village.

'Thank you, sir. Sir, one smoke please,' the driver begged. Arjun obliged and passed him one, and lit it for him. The driver relished the quality, being more accustomed to a cheaper brand. He smiled with gratitude and restarted the rickshaw to head off.

'Wait, take these.' Arjun passed over his cigarette box and lighter to the driver. 'Enjoy.' He had decided not to take a chance: a flicker from the lighter or the smell of cigarette smoke could give away his presence.

As the rickshaw turned and drove off, Arjun stepped into the shadows, out of the moonlight. The dog padded along behind him, coming to take a closer look at the stranger who had invaded his village in the night. Arjun paid him off with an apple from his bag, and he was allowed to continue. About twenty-five metres ahead was the missionary gate. Arjun had no intention of going to the main entrance, but instead meandered around the back of the building until he found a set of steps by a derelict building.

He climbed up to the top and found a spot with a view of the mission and the grassland beyond, reaching down to the riverbank. There was little to see in the shadows: the village was asleep, unaware a watchful eye had arrived. He crouched down, opened his bag and pulled out a second apple. He had a dozen more inside. He brought out a gun wrapped in cloth, and a magazine of bullets, and placed both on the cloth. The last item was his binoculars. He peered through the lenses and scoured the rooftops and alleyways below. Still nothing to see.

He sat back against the terrace, loaded the gun with six rounds of bullets and held the gun out. Felt its weight and firmed his grip. It had been a while since he'd held a gun; in this job, he had more use of a pen to strike down his enemy. He held the gun across his chest, his fingers twitching for a cigarette, but he had none.

The mist breathed slowly across the forest canopy. Trees spiked through the greyish wash. Beneath them Nana slept uneasily besides the fire. His head hurt; his mouth was dry; his eyes pulled in as he found himself tortured in his dream. He saw himself beside the same fire, at night, entombed by the swirling mist. He saw himself woken by whispers leaching from the forest, whispers calling him by name: 'Nana... Nana.' The calls came from all sides as he spun around. The calls grew louder and louder with each turn he made, voices of girls calling his name, their words seeping inside his head. He covered his ears and cried out: 'Leave me alone, leave me alone!'

He broke out of his dream and found himself stooping in the mist.

Confronted by darkness, he picked up a flaming stick from the fire and turned a full circle. The flame wavered from side to side as he searched for the voices. A growl caught his attention: it was heading his way through the forest. He could just make out the cracking of branches and the rustle of leaves; it was near. Nana tried to step back, but found his retreat halted by a second growl from behind him, which was followed by others, coming from all sides of the forest.

Nana stood still. If this was a dream, it was a bad one – but it wasn't, he was awake, alone in the mist with whatever it was coming for him. He turned a full circle, holding the flaming branch, but there was nothing to see.

'Nana...' a girl's voice cried. 'Nana.'

He turned, but there was no girl. The voice came again from another side. Again he looked and again there was no girl.

'Have you come for me?' he shouted. 'Then take me!' He threw the log away and raised his hands. If this was his time, he feared nothing.

'Take me,' he pleaded. 'Take me.'

The voices kept coming, torturing his mind. He fell to his knees and bowed his head: he was defeated and tired.

'Take me.'

Once more the voices vanished. He sat up and looked into the dark, and this time he was met by eyes – dozens of eyes, red in colour, cutting through the stillness, on all sides, creeping closer and closer. The eyes grew bigger.

'Take me...' Nana begged once more, and the eyes pounced.

All went quiet. He found himself alone once more in the dark. Apart from his pounding heart and heavy breathing, the forest was asleep. He lowered his guard. The fire guttered. He was mistaken; it had been a dream.

An hour passed then Nana woke, covered in sweat. The forest was asleep once more. No more whispers, there were no more eyes; the fire was dead. He washed his face.

SIXTY-EIGHT

The hours passed slowly as the sky turned from black to blue and then awoke to a crimson morning. Life crept in with the milkman's arrival in front of the mission gate. His call was loud, and broke what little sleep Arjun had found. He enjoyed a feast of two more apples, then turned to gaze across the village and finally down to the mission, where a flood of children arrived at a brisk pace. They were in good spirits, at least for today, Maya's loss set aside for a day. Today was Choti Holi, the day before the much-celebrated colour festival of Holi. It was a day of fires and of sacrifice, celebrating the triumph of good over evil in times of myth and legend.

Every year the mission children built the biggest bonfire of the village, a custom started by Agatha when she first joined the mission. It was her way of bonding with the villagers and their traditions. Today was no different. Arjun looked on as the children spent the day carting back and forth stacks of broken branches. A mighty stack rose at the centre of a plateau overlooking the river. Arjun watched as the day passed. He failed to notice someone else watching him back, from the river. A fisherman sat on the prow of his boat, his face shielded by a cloth to keep out the flies that danced over the water. He'd spent much of the day anchored in the river, close to a bend, occasionally steering a few metres up and down then anchoring once again. For his efforts he'd only managed to net a small catch of tilapia. But he wasn't interested in the fish, and neither was he a fisherman. It was Nana – biding his time, watching, waiting close by. He was too far away to be seen by Arjun, and looked like a fisherman going about his business. Nana played his part, giving nothing away: he was waiting for the sun to set and for the fires to light.

As the sun set Nana steered his boat upstream and moored it away from the bonfire. He was met by a woodsman who had carted freshly cut wood, with the help of a bullock. The delivery met with Nana's satisfaction. The wood was unloaded and stacked to form a pyre. The man handed over some other items Nana had requested, and then left, along with his dinner, a bucket load of tilapia.

During the first hour of darkness Nana washed in the water and put on fresh clothes he'd bought with some of Kasi's money. He combed his long hair, and scented it with oils that shone in the emerging moonlight. He looked radiant, ready to finish what his student had started.

This was the longest time Arjun had gone without cigarettes. His fingers tapped. He tried to focus on a tune, but his fingers couldn't follow the rhythm, itching instead to hold a rolled-up cigarette. He regretted giving his smokes away. A loud cheer from the bonfire gave him a much-needed distraction. Arjun lifted the binoculars to take a look. Through them he could make out the children throwing rags onto the bonfire. Each throw met with applause and cheers from the gathered crowd, a mix of children from the mission and local villagers. Helen was among them, helping a young girl steady her arms at a safe distance from the fire, before she flung her rags into the flames. The rags burned and fuelled the bonfire on, the flame climbing higher. Sacrificing the old to be replaced by the new – a sacrifice that a child could understand and the poor could manage. It was like shedding your skin for a new one, burning old sins away, to be reborn without sin – a new start that the city would celebrate tonight, with the eruption of colours on the next day.

Arjun gave a rare smile, remembering his own days as a child on the ghats, and the bonfires around Assi that had been lit by his father. He remembered his father's dismay when he found his mother throwing his favourite old shirt in the fire. It was tatty, full of holes but cosy and fitted to his father's figure. It was like an old friend. His father always gave in in the end and let the shirt burn, for he had learned to sacrifice what was dear to him, to give meaning to its loss: the greater the loss, the greater the sacrifice. Arjun was so busy thinking about his past in the reflection of the children's joy around the bonfire that he missed something happening close by.

'Helen, Helen,' Nana called – gentle words, spoken as he kept out of sight. He was just below the flat lands, on the mud bank. Helen eventually heard his familiar voice and came down to greet him.

'Nana, what are you doing down there? Come up here, join us.' She extended her hand to pull him up. He didn't extend his.

'I've just come to say goodbye, Helen. I'm leaving and, well, I just wanted to see you one more time and give you a departing gift. It's not valuable, but I hope it's something you'll remember me by.' He then extended his left hand, his right firmly behind his back in the darkness.

'Please come I've kept it for you in the boat.'

She leaned over and could see the blinking light of the lantern in the fishing boat, down below.

'Please, let me help you down.' He stepped back to give her space and to make sure she was totally out of sight behind the vines and bushes. She grabbed his left hand for support as she skidded towards him.

'It's fine, I've got you,' he said, leading her forward, and swung down his right hand. Clenched in his fist was a thick wooden branch. He hit her on the neck and knocked her out cold, catching her before she fell. He made his way down to the riverbank, Helen, unconscious, over his shoulder. He picked up the lantern from the boat and vanished downstream.

Arjun scanned across the crowd, then noticed that Helen was missing. He looked harder, covering all the angles, and she remained missing. He got up and looked again and saw Agatha wandering around – she was looking for someone.

'Helen,' Arjun muttered. He picked up his phone and gun. The mobile was dead. He threw it down and headed down the steps. Running through the dark alleys, he tripped and tumbled on the uneven cobbled path, twisting his foot.

'Shit, shit!' He felt the pain and his ankle swelled up. He picked himself up and tried to run, but the ankle slowed him to a crawl.

Along the riverbank, Nana left fresh footprints in the mud as he made his way to the stack of wood – an unlit pyre soaked in petrol, inches from the river. An occasional breath of wind pushed the river to skim the logs at the pyre's base. The creak of the oil lantern grew louder as Nana approached the pyre.

'Helen – where is Helen?' Arjun made his way through the crowds.

'Arjun, when did you get here?' Agatha asked.

'Helen, where is she?' he hastily replied, then she noticed the gun in his hand.

'My God, what's happened?'

Arjun leaned over the bush to look down at the river. There was enough moonlight to make out the marks of Helen's skid down the mud bank, and the faint outline of the fishing boat below. Arjun fought the heat of the fire, grabbed a burning log from the bonfire and made his way down the mud bank. He bit back his pain and moved as fast as he could: finding the trail of footprints spurred him faster. He held the gun out in front of him.

Nana placed Tulsi in Helen's mouth. He paused to fix her face in his memory. The pendant hanging around her neck, the silver Tulsi threaded around the emerald stone, bolstered his belief – and Kasi's – that her sacrifice had been ordained by the gods. It was her time to die, her karma. Two clay pots rested next to the pyre, filled with oil. Nana emptied the oil from one over her clothes, and left enough to lace his fingers with and rub through her hair. As he stroked her hair, her eyes twitched. It was time.

Nana smashed the lantern on the pyre, which erupted with flames. Arjun spotted the flames as he turned the bend, and found Nana inches from the pyre, Helen stretched out in his arms, ready to be sacrificed.

'What are you waiting for?' Nana asked Arjun, sensing he was just behind him.

'Nana, put her down. You don't need to do this.' Arjun eased a foot closer, then another, buying time with his plea.

'You'll never understand. I'm freeing her from this life, from her pain.'

'You're killing her for Kasi, aren't you? She's the final sacrifice for him, your student.'

'Don't come any closer. I'll fall into the fire with her. Stop. Throw the gun away – do it now!' Nana demanded.

Arjun hesitated but he knew Nana meant it. As Nana leaned forward into the heat, the flames singed the hairs on his skin and Helen's arm, hanging down, jerked as the heat burned her into consciousness. Her shirt caught alight as the flames reached out.

Arjun threw the gun into the dirt and got ready to jump Nana.

'He's played you, Nana, your student played you. You're doing his dirty work – you, the master, doing Kasi's bidding. That makes you his student, Nana, Kasi's student.' He inched closer.

'Shut up! You know nothing. I am the master.'

Helen's arm swung up as she regained consciousness. She reached up and bit Nana's shoulder. He lost his hold and she fell. Her shirt alight, she rolled over and over in the mud and put the flames out.

'Helen…' he cried out. 'Helen.'

Arjun jumped him. The two tussled in the ground, rolled, then broke apart. Arjun looked for the gun. Nana seized the second pot and threw the oil over Arjun as he scavenged in the dirt for his gun. Nana grabbed a burning log and thrust it towards Arjun. He saw the gun at the same time, but Helen was nearer to it than he was.

'Helen... the gun, take it,' he shouted to her. She could barely see, still dazed from the clubbing she'd received. He shouted again, and tripped as his ankle gave way beneath him. Nana jumped on him. Arjun held his arms off, the burning log, dripping with flame, inches from his petrol-laced face. Nana relished the fight: his eyes lit up, raging with delight.

'Helen, help me, Helen!' This time she responded, and crawled through the dirt and found the gun. Her hands shook as she gripped it with both hands and pointed it at the figures in front of her.

A flame flared across Arjun's face. The petrol caught fire, and his glasses protected his sight as his skin burned. He pushed Nana back, wiping the flames from his face, but his shirt was also alight.

'Shoot, Helen, shoot,' he cried. Nana's clothes caught alight.

Helen moved the gun from figure to figure: neither was clear, darkened against the fires of the pyre behind. The two tugged at each other. Arjun closed in, ignored the pain, braced himself in the mud and pushed Nana hard. His ploy failed as Nana swung round and Arjun found himself facing the fire. His clothes flamed, and he cried out in pain. The flames spread from his shirt to Nana's – now both were on fire. Neither gave way as the fires took hold.

'Helen, shoot him, shoot him now!'

She fired.

The gunshot made her stagger back. Her injured neck hit a boulder, and she passed out again.

The pyre raged without mercy, feasting on flesh – one of the men had fallen. Hit by the bullet, the body smashed into the burning wood and cooked in its flames. The survivor, alight with flames, stumbled away and plunged into the river. The water eased the pain of his burns, and he struggled beneath the tide in the silt waters. One hand pierced the surface as he moved with the water. Then his face emerged from the water and he gasped for air. He kept moving, barely holding himself above the water, being carried along by the current beyond the bend, the funeral pyre burning like a distant star. He passed the plateau, glowing with its giant bonfire, and his hands fought to keep himself above the water. His body ached as parts of his charred skin stung and peeled away.

Upstream, the fire raged as the sacrifice crisped and smouldered. Other pyres, far away, across the old city, burned their last flames. When midnight struck, Choti Holi was over. The sacrifice was over, and everyone filtered back to their homes. Varanasi fell silent, the pyres died, and faint stars could be seen once more, straddling the skyline.

SIXTY-NINE

By morning's light, a herd of police jeeps and motorcycles had camped on the rise of the riverbank, overlooking the Varuna. Inside one jeep, slouched on the front passenger seat, was Helen, still shivering under a blanket. Her eyes were dazed, oblivious to her surroundings, her face rested against the door: she was a lost soul, unable to remember what had happened the night before.

Along the riverbank, the police, led by Tripathi, searched through the remains of the funeral pyre. Only a few bone fragments remained among the ash. Nothing of notable form, like a skull, was left. The fire had destroyed everything. Tripathi waved to the police officers on the two fishing boats. Along with the fisherman, they poked wooden rods into the river in search of a body. Two other fisherman took turns to dive under the water, but they found nothing.

'Anything?' shouted Tripathi. The answer was as it had been for the past hour: nothing.

His police radio buzzed. He raised it to his ear. It was Mehra.

'Did you find him?' he asked.

'No sir, nothing yet. The girl doesn't remember much. She remembers waking up in front of the fire, there was some kind of struggle between Arjun and Nana, and then she fired the gun – a single shot, as far as she could remember. She saw someone fall into the fire and someone else limp into the river. But who was who, she has no idea. She passed out soon afterwards. I'm sending her in. Sir, I'm going to need more men.'

Tripathi crouched down to sift through the ash, unsure whether he was looking at the remains of Arjun or Nana.

SEVENTY

With little traffic on the roads, the police jeep crossed the bridge and entered the old city. Helen sat in the front passenger seat. She'd said nothing through the ride, failing to respond to polite questions from the police driver and the accompanying female officer in the back. Both of them tried their best to trigger a conversation with her, but failed to get a single word out of her as she gripped the side bar and stared straight ahead.

The driver veered off the main road at Assi, and instead of taking the highway around the old city, took a shortcut. Within minutes of entering the narrow lane, he came across a crowd of local teenagers, students and locals among them, dancing and throwing coloured powder into the air and at one another. The police jeep was in the middle of a human rainbow, jolting and jumping as splashes of different coloured powder rained down and covered the faces waiting below. It was the final, and most celebrated, day of the Holi festival. With the sacrifice over the night before, today was about music and celebration, and the boys of Assi had come alive, chanting their favourite dance lyrics to the deafening beat of an oil drum, brought alive by a wooden stick hitting its sides.

The driver blasted the horn in vain. A powder bomb smashed against the front window, obscuring the view with a reddish coating. It jerked Helen out of her self-imposed daze, as the crowds swarmed around the jeep and in front of her. Another blast of colours hit her side of the jeep, marking her face with lashings of red, green, blue and yellow dust. She wiped it from her eyelashes and watched the heaving swell of happy-go-lucky boys and men.

The driver flicked the wipers on, washing a clear area on the front window. Between the swishing wiper blades, Helen saw him. Far back, behind the crowds, she saw Nana! His eyes were unmistakable, holding hers, and a shudder ran down her spine. Like the others, he was covered in colours, but that didn't hide his eyes. As others danced all around him, those eyes never once flinched. Helen stared back, her face close to the window. He was still standing there. Then a wave of hands crisscrossed in front of her and the drum beat became louder as the drummer jumped onto the jeep. The officer stepped out from his side, to clear a path for the jeep. When Helen looked back into the crowd, Nana had gone.

From inside the car she heard the sound of stray dogs barking on the terrace running along the footpath wall. The dogs, two of them, looked at her, then back towards the crowds, barking louder and louder with each drum beat. Helen stepped out of the car as the dogs ran along the terrace. Occasionally turning back to her, they seemed to be calling her, guiding her to follow them.

'Miss… Miss,' the female officer called out as Helen strayed into the crowds. She covered her ears as the pounding beat assaulted her ear drums. The face of the drummer, bright and cheerful, egged her on, to dance, to jump, to let go.

Thrown from side to side by the sheer force of other bodies pushing and pounding with the rhythm, she found herself moving through the crowds without any control. A hand swung up and thumped her ear: she felt numb and lost hearing in that ear. Her eyes wandered in all directions, dizzied by the swirling crowds, but she regained her concentration and found the dogs waiting for her on the terrace. They jumped, barking, as Helen made it through the worse of the crowds. She was covered in powder, like everyone else, and brushed it off. The dogs, a few metres in front of her, waited for her. Behind them lay a narrow spiral staircase leading to the Ganges. To the side of the entrance was a small temple under the branches of a banyan tree. Several wreaths of fresh Tulsi lay inside the temple arch. The words inscribed into the stone beneath marked the ghat's name: *Tulsi Ghat*. Trailing back from the stone, watery footprints, freshly marked with red colouring, disappeared down the steps. The dogs headed down and Helen went with them, the sides of the wall marked by the brushing of fingertips covered in red colouring. On the steps or across the walls, the marking led her to the final step and onto the riverbank. The sun held steady on the horizon as the river beneath flowed by. The dogs stepped into the water, barking and barking. The footprints continued over the muddy silt.

Helen looked across the river. Where had he gone? she wondered. Those eyes, so distinct, had brought her here; she noticed the stray dogs, which appeared to be disturbed by something in the river as they continued to howl towards it, but there was no one to be found, just footprints fading into the water. Having followed the dogs in, Helen found herself in the river, and the Ganges washed over her skin.

'Miss... Miss, come back,' said the female officer, making her way onto the bank. Helen turned and found her, but the dogs kept barking – whatever had spooked them was still there, on the river, around them.

'You must come with me.' The officer led her out and back onto the bank. To one side, beyond the moored boats, the frail old man sat as he had always done on his wooden seat. In front of him, two men were busy building a funeral pyre. The elderly man was dead. His hands were clasped in prayer, even though the life within him had gone.

'We must go.' The officer led Helen up the steps. Turning for a brief glimpse back, she found the dogs still playing in the shallows, still barking. She continued to hear them until the pounding beat of the oil drums took over once again.

Helen was nudged aside as a priest hurried by, bringing with him a holy flame to light the pyre. She watched the elderly man's corpse be placed on top on the pyre. The priest lit the wood and straw at the base. A trail of wooden boats drifted nearby, and on board, eager tourists leaned over, briefly tipping the boat to one side as they focused their cameras on the pyre. The marigold flowers draped over the red cloth were the first to wilt in the rising heat, followed by the white cloth, which singed and disappeared as the flames engulfed it.

'Ma'am?' The officer tugged at Helen's hand. It was time to leave. Unsure of what she'd seen – had it been Nana or not? – her eyes searched for him, but there was nothing to explain it. So she let go and left, leaving the dogs behind. Several circled the pyre, howling as the flames rose. There was no one left to mourn. The priest left, along with the two helpers, leaving the pyre to burn, accompanied by howls.

SEVENTY-ONE

Two Weeks Later – New Delhi, CBI Headquarters

Like it was every Monday morning, the highway was gridlocked. The sound of horns echoed up from the street, but didn't reach the higher floors. It was much quieter there. Ms Mirza, the floor's secretary, was busy inside Arjun's office. While officers' faces changed, she was a permanent fixture. The order had come down from upstairs. She had been asked to clear the room before the new tenant made an appearance. Thankfully, he was running late – no doubt caught up in the traffic – giving Ms Mirza a few extra minutes to pack Arjun's final box. She'd taken longer than necessary, taking care to pack each of Arjun's personal items neatly. Though they'd worked on the same floor together for three years, he'd never once asked her first name, always referring to her as Ms Mirza, and that's how she liked it, being impersonal by nature. She left the most important item to the end. It was a small, dark blue velvet box. She held it and opened it. Inside there was a polished bronze medal.

'Good morning,' said Virdas Kumar. Arjun's replacement had arrived. He slammed his suitcase onto the desk, along with a bundle of wrapped flowers, and leaned over to the window. He pulled the blinds up to let in the light, transforming the room from a dimly lit space to one that was more sterile and in keeping with the other offices.

'That's better! So you must be Ms Mirza? These are for you.' He passed her the flowers. He had the keenness of a freshly promoted officer. Virdas was well groomed, with polished shoes and a neatly knotted tie.

He noticed the medal.

'I thought it would be bigger.'

Two weeks had passed since Holi, and the local force had found nothing. Forensic examination of bone fragments from the pyre had come back negative; what bone pieces remained had fused in the heat. There was no DNA or dental records for Arjun or Nana, and both were still missing. The local force had moved on, and the now it was the CBI's turn. The medal – a final reward for Arjun's effort – remained in his office, but there was no family to collect it. Ms Mirza placed it inside the box, at the top, and sealed it.

'Where will you take it?' Virdas asked as he sat down in Arjun's old chair. It creaked as he shuffled to get comfortable. 'I'm going to need a new chair.'

Ms Mirza left, ignoring him. She passed the box to the porter.

'So that's how it ends,' Virdas muttered as he watched her.

All that CBI Arjun Das had had in his office was in a cardboard box, heading to storage.

SEVENTY-TWO

Police Station, Varanasi

Tripathi hesitated on the final line of his report. He only needed to type in today's date, but he held back. It didn't sit well with him, closing the file. He knew what it meant putting down a closing date: it made things official. After that, files were rarely reopened. It was also his last report for the station. He'd disobeyed Mehra in favour of Arjun. The price he had paid was a reassignment to a smaller police station. But he didn't mind: it was a rural setting close to the village where he'd grown up. Life would slow down, as not much happened in rural areas, except for the occasional brawl between farmers.

He decided to leave off the date and rolled out the sheet, stacked the pages neatly together, and placed them inside a file. He said a final goodbye to his desk – he wasn't coming back after his last meeting with Mehra.

'Can I come in, sir?' He knocked on Mehra's door.

'Make it quick,' Mehra replied in an unfriendly tone. Without so much as a glance at Tripathi, he tapped on his desk, to indicate where he should leave the file. Tripathi put the file down, opened it and made one last effort to engage Mehra.

'Sir, there's been a report of a new sighting of someone matching Nana's description. Should it be looked into, sir?'

But Mehra was silent. Instead, he pulled the file in front of him. Rather than read it, he went straight to the back page, where he noticed the date was missing. He filled it in and then stamped the file with his official marker.

Tripathi couldn't help but notice a crisp front-page copy of the local newspaper hanging in pride of place next to the Indian flag. One headline read *DCP MEHRA ENDS SERIAL KILLER TERROR*. Another read *DCP MEHRA BEATS CBI*, and a third read *MEHRA KILLS SERIAL KILLER*. There was nothing more rewarding than a good ending, and Mehra had his in print. He was a rising star in Varanasi now: a political office was in reach, and with the press on his side he wasn't going to ruin his chances.

'Sirjee?' Mehra called his assistant in. He passed him the file and told him where it should go. 'Basement.'

Tripathi left without so much as a goodbye from Mehra. He stepped outside to a waiting police jeep, which had been sent from his new posting to collect him. The young officer in the driving seat asked his permission to leave.

'Is everything here?' Tripathi asked.

'Yes, sir. The box is the back.'

Tripathi turned to take a look, and peered inside the box. It was all there: several files, inside them copies of the key case notes. He pulled out a folded set of papers from inside his jacket and straightened them out. He'd made a copy of his last report before passing it to Mehra. There was no date on the final page. He placed it in the box and asked the driver to move on.

As May arrived, the landscape changed. There was more dust in the air as the soil dried in the unforgiving heat. The Ganges narrowed – steps that had been hidden beneath the waters reappeared, and made uncomfortably hot seating spots. It was time for tourists to leave. Tripathi had ventured back to the forest where Nana had lived, as he'd done every weekend since leaving. Each time he came back hoping to find new evidence of Nana's reappearance. He'd spend hours roaming around nearby farms and local villages, sharing evening tea with farmers. On occasion he'd learn about a roaming priest who fitted Nana's description, and he'd investigate it further, only to come up against another dead end. But he carried on, and one Friday evening his persistence paid off.

His name was Suki Singh, and he was the cousin of a local farmer Tripathi had met a few weeks earlier. Suki had shared stories of a miracle man with his cousin, who told

Tripathi about them. Suki was from a village on the edge of Rajdari, a lush forest with a mighty waterfall and gorge cutting deep through its heart. It was a few hours south of Varanasi, for anyone catching a ride on a passing lorry.

Over tea and snacks, Suki shared the rumours of the miracle man's work. Although he had had no direct contact with him, and had not witnessed any of the wonders he'd heard about, Tripathi sensed Suki believed everything he had heard. Rumours turned into fact, so strong was his retelling of what others had said. Tripathi took a chance and showed him the photographs of Nana, but since he had never seen him, it proved a wasted effort. But Suki offered up something more than tales and whispers; he gave a specific location. He'd heard the priest lived inside one of the caves found beneath the gorge, where the waterfall threw up a misty spray that shielded the cave entrance from outsiders. With the rising heat, the water had slowed, and the cave was visible.

'I want you to take me there,' Tripathi said. Suki agreed, but he didn't expect to go so soon.

'Now.' Tripathi stood up. Suki was reluctant to rush back; he had only just arrived. Tripathi kept it simple and flashed his police badge. It did the trick: Suki agreed, but requested that his cousin come with them. The three left and crossed the iron bridge at speed. In his eagerness to get there, Tripathi overtook lorries and bullocks, at times scraping his jeep's sides – it was already tatty and pounded with hits, so a few more would do nothing to its value. Within an hour and half they had arrived, his speed cutting the journey time by half. Tripathi kept his pistol loaded, and followed Suki through the forest and down to the waterfall. The rocks were covered in a slippery coating of water and moss: in the dark, one false step could prove fatal. Carefully, the three climbed down beside the waterfall, rock by rock, a torch providing a little light. When they reached the bottom, Suki stopped, refusing to go any further. He wasn't the one with the gun, and like the rest of the villagers he wasn't about to confront a miracle man, especially at this late hour. He pointed to the opening ahead – a small clearing between rocks. There was no direct path to it; the only way was through the water. Knee-deep in cold water, Tripathi made his way to the entrance, holding his pistol in one hand and the unlit torch in another. He didn't want to alert anyone he was outside.

He stepped out of the water and stood in the darkness, listening to the echoing of the waterfall. He held his pistol in front of him and walked into the cave, then he flicked the torch on. The flash of light spread across the cave as he moved the torch around. The cave was empty. He moved in further, exploring, but there was only one way out – the way he had come in. He put his pistol away and continued to look around with the torch. His reward came when he found a pile of rocks against a rock face. Someone had arranged them to hold a fire – burned ash lay in the centre. Behind the rocks, etched on the cave wall he found words. He couldn't read them; they were written in Sanskrit. He took a photograph of them with his phone. In the morning, a priest in Varanasi translated them for him. They read *TO HAVE NOTHING, IS EVERYTHING.*

SEVENTY-THREE

London in May was a world away from Varanasi.

'We'll shortly be commencing our descent before landing,' the captain announced over the tannoy as the plane cast its shadow over the restless waters of the English Channel.

Helen, having failed to sleep for most of the flight, had finally fallen into a deep sleep. It took the air hostess three attempts to wake her, and the last only worked because she pinched her. Helen's seat was in the wrong position, and needed to be put upright. Dazed, she simply let the air hostess adjust the seat for her. It was only when the Indian passenger next to her, in the window seat, shared her excitement on seeing the landmarks of London appear below them that she realised she was home.

'I can see the dome,' the passenger said. 'You must be glad to be home?'

'Home,' Helen yawned. 'Home…' she smiled back. 'Yes, I'm glad to be home.'

She took the taxi home from the airport. Cutting through the suburban roads, she remembered what Agatha had said: *the unfamiliar became familiar.* As she looked through the foggy window, the world outside had – strangely – become unfamiliar and distant.

'We're here, Miss,' said the taxi driver as he pulled off the main road and parked outside her flat.

As she unlocked the front door, the phone was ringing inside. She dropped her bags and went for the phone. The display showed a number: the prefix '91' meant the caller was in India. She answered.

'Hello… hello?'

But there was no response, just the sound of breathing, soft and calming. There was someone there – she could make out the faint sound of traffic, not busy, but like a truck driving down a highway.'Hello…' she said again. 'Is that you, Agatha?' She hadn't quite got used to calling Agatha her mother. 'Agatha? Agatha? Hello?'

Still no answer. Helen put the phone down. As she sat on the bed the phone rang again, and when she answered she was again met with the same silence. She put the phone down and checked the list of missed calls on the phone's display. The same number had rung five times in the past hour.

Helen dialled back. After a pause while the long-distance line connected, and she heard a faint ringtone. No one answered for the first minute, but she held on for a while longer. Just as she was about to put the phone down, someone answered.

'*Kaun*,' said a voice. This was Hindi for 'who', but Helen didn't understand.

'Hello?' she said.

The voice of a man replied: 'Hello?' It turned out he was the owner of a roadside café off the highway, a few kilometres west of Rajdari.

'English – do you speak English?' Helen asked in desperation.

'Little,' he replied.

'You rang my number several times. It's Helen from London.'

'Helen? No, I not ring you.' He turned to another man who was sipping tea beside him. 'I don't understand what she wants,' he confessed to him in Hindi. 'Some foreign lady calling from London. Did anyone call from here to an English lady?' he asked the customers scattered around his café. There was no reply.

'Hello? Hello, are you calling from the mission?' Helen asked.

'No,' the man replied. One of the customers pointed to a man walking away from the café. He told the owner that the man had been the last one to use the phone.

The owner looked down the highway; the man was barely visible in the dusty haze.

'Miss, wait, wait – checking,' he told Helen.

The café owner walked down the track along the highway and shouted out, 'Hey! Hey, there's a call for you. Hey… there's a phone call from London.' His heavy body weighed him down.

The man ahead didn't turn. He kept walking as the café owner tried to close the gap. At the sound of an approaching truck, the man turned and hailed it. He glanced at the breathless café owner still some distance away, but took no notice of him. The truck pulled in and the man got in.

'How far are you going?' the man asked the driver as the truck pulled away.

'All the way to Delhi,' the driver replied.

'By the way, I'm Sid.' The driver offered his hand in welcome.

'Nana,' the man replied. 'My name's Nana.' He'd shed his ragged clothes and untidy look for a clean shave, shirt and trousers. He was ready for Delhi.

Helen hung up. As she sat on the bed she noticed Sarah's oil painting of Varanasi on the wall. She gazed across at the painting, from the mass of bathers washing in the Ganges, to the burning funeral fires and then to the far right corner, where her eye was drawn to a lone man sitting, unconcerned, as a pyre burned by his side. She got off the bed and picked up the painting to take a closer look. She noticed the man was covered in ash and behind him there were dogs, several of them, running towards him, howling. The man in the painting appeared to stare back at her. It reminded her of *him*. Helen whispered his name.

'Nana.'

The Rishi Scrolls

BOOK ONE

FALL OF ARYA

RAJAN KUMAR PATEL

There is something beneath the snow, something old and forgotten. Buried deep within the borderless snow-draped mountains of the Himalayas, the ruins of an ancient kingdom remain hidden from the world under an ocean of ice. Its history faded into myth and legend and its name unspoken for thousands of years. This is the tale of this place – its Kings, its battles, its time of glory, its reign in between the histories of the Ramayana and the Mahabharata. Its legacy confined to my memory alone. This is the story of the Kingdom of Arya.

And I am Aryan; an echo from it's past, a Prince of Arya. An immortal, I have lived more lifetimes than I care to remember. There is no sea I have not sailed; no tribe I have not shared bread with. I was there when a carpenter was crucified and a Christian was born. I have drunk wine with Alexander in the Hindu Kush and followed Gandhi's shadow as he marched to the Salt mines of Dhandi. I have watched the sun rise for a million days and seen empires fall into shadow. I have seen all that I have loved fade into darkness. Walking the earth in solitude, waiting for the day that was foretold to me: when the seeds of Arya would rise again and I would be reunited with old friends. That day has finally come. It is time for the sleepers to awaken.

EXCLUSIVE CHAPTER

Master of the swift sword

Tokyo, Japan – Present Day

Six years had passed since Hiro had lost his father, and each year, on the anniversary of his father's death, he passed the day polishing a small silver pocket watch. The silver sheen of the casing never failed to catch his attention when his father had flicked it open, leaving the teenager wondering how such a small thing held sway over his father's time.

Hiro stared at the watch face, catching his reflection in the glass as he remembered the last time he saw his father. A few days before his tenth birthday, his father was packing his suitcase; he was leaving, duty before family. It wasn't the first time he'd missed his son's birthday, but to make amends he'd decided to give Hiro a special gift, something his own father had passed to him when he was the same age.

'I'd like to borrow your watch,' he said as he knelt down to his boy and held his arm, with his watch in sight. 'I promise I'll take good care of it.'

He then pulled out a soft white napkin from inside his jacket, placed it in Hiro's hand and opened it. The pocket watch lay inside. It had never shone so bright as it did that day.

'It's yours now.' They exchanged watches – Hiro's yellow plastic one for his father's handmade silver pocket watch. His father wore the plastic watch with great pride, even though it looked out of place with his uniform. Hiro wasn't to know it would be the last time he would see his father – and his watch. That evening, as the light faded and the stars gave life to the night sky, Hiro and his mother watched from the docks and waved goodbye as his father's naval ship slipped quietly out to sea.

Hiro's father served as a warrant officer on board a Japanese naval destroyer and, like five generations of men in his family, his first love was the sea. The might of the ocean expanse was an open book, with each day as unpredictable as the next. Sea water flowed in his veins; it also claimed his life. The naval accident report stated that Warrant Officer Isamu was lost at sea. His body was never recovered.

What was meant to be a routine rescue drill turned fatal as the sea's mood abruptly changed. Isamu was stranded with two other sailors on board a lifeboat as winds and tides lashed them from all sides. The ship's captain, a confident brute, ordered the drill to continue. It was his first commission, and he put his personal pride before the crew's safety. Only when Isamu was thrown into the heaving sea did the captain heed the call for help and send in a rescue boat, but for Isamu it was too late.

During the inquest the naval command closed ranks and blamed Isamu for his fate. Hiro's mother tried to speak out, telling the panel it was easy to blame everything on Isamu. 'He's dead,' she said. 'The silent have no defenders, just the tears of a weeping widow seeking justice.'

Her outbursts were unwelcome and quickly quelled. She knew the moment she stepped into the inquest chamber that the men, grey-haired and seated upright and stern on the panel, had already made their minds up. The rest was purely for show, and before she embarrassed them further they politely escorted her out of the room. They were always polite; that's how they defeated her. The press, as usual, only remembered the outbursts, never the silence of a grieving window.

Left outside the chamber doors, she realised how small her world was – just the two of them. She and her son. She knelt down and looked straight at Hiro.

'Promise me you'll have nothing to do with the navy – promise me, Hiro.' He often dreamed of being at sea at his father's side, and one day joining the ranks of the navy like the men before him. Isamu would have wanted the same. But he was gone. Hiro was all his mother had, and he wasn't about to break his mother's heart.

'I promise,' he said, holding her tightly.

The bell rang outside his window. It was six o'clock. Hiro placed the watch back into the napkin and headed to the window. From his first-floor view, in his modest apartment, he stared through the soot towards the dark alley across the street. He pressed his face against the cold skin of the window; it made him feel alive.

The alley was wafer-thin and deep, shielded on either side by rising tower blocks that defined the world around him. He looked along the alley, as he did each day, waiting for him. A sudden burst of sunlight washed through the alley, filling it with a blinding glare. Hiro looked back, catching a glimpse of the setting sun at the far end. Then he appeared, piercing through the golden haze, first his shadow, then the man – his friend the Samurai.

Hiro watched the Samurai graciously stride to the centre of the street, where he stopped within sight of the Underground station a hundred metres in front. The Samurai was a relic of a glorious past: a warrior, poised to fight without fear, standing firm on the battlefield. Waiting for the enemy to rise and meet him for a fight he longed would one day claim his life and free him with a honourable death.

His stillness was deceptive. To the untrained eye, he looked like a statue, but Hiro looked beyond the stillness, and saw the Samurai's finger flick open the thin buckle of his sword scabbard, drawing out no more than an inch of steel.

The Samurai's feet were braced against the tarmac; he raised his brow, sensing a tremor coming his way. He turned and looked up to Hiro – he knew he was watching – and they shared a respectful look. A gust of wind blew through. Hiro felt the window shake: the enemy had arrived. The Samurai turned to face them.

An army of black suits poured out from the station and headed straight for him. He gripped his sword and yelled out a warning – a final reprieve, but none heeded him as they marched on. He raised his sword to strike as the suits split and passed around him, leaving him alone on his tarmac island. The Samurai kept up the theatre as hundreds of people passed by until one lone suit, a young office clerk, bowed to him and gestured an invitation to join him for dinner at the noodle bar across the street. The show was over. The Samurai looked back at Hiro with a knowing smile; dinner was fixed. That evening the bars came alive with the chattering of men in suits drowning their souls in cheap warm sake in the hope they would forget the passing of another tedious day. As for the young office clerk, his head was filled with the Samurai's tales as he relived a past he would never see.

Rain or shine, on the hour, the Samurai gave the same performance without fail at the end of each day, dressed in his flawless dark blue kimono and carrying a blunt steel sword. The passing suits saw him as a harmless reflection of their common past.

The Samurai had a mortal name: Mr Kawasaki. He had first met Hiro the day after he had moved into the apartment with his mother. The local boys teamed up to taunt the new boy on the block, and it wasn't long before a fight broke out. Even outnumbered seven to one, Hiro fought back. Mr Kawasaki watched the scuffle from a far, eager to see how well the boy fared. Hiro put up a worthy fight and it wasn't a lack of courage that brought him down, but the constant blows from fourteen hands. Out-thumped and exhausted, it was time for Mr Kawasaki to step in. Armed with a walking stick, he struck a single blow, bringing down one of the seven, who lay – out cold – on the ground. The rest scattered, smart enough to know the fight was over.

In the days that followed the Samurai and the new boy became friends, one watching the other at six o'clock. To the masses Mr Kawasaki was just a performer, an old quack, spinning tales of Samurai adventures to passers-by who needed the company and could pay his price – a single bowl of hot chicken noodle soup. But Hiro saw only a Samurai before him: he believed him to be a veteran of the last war, a man of honour, a man like his father.

The two bonded as student and master. Mr Kawasaki trained Hiro to be like him, a Samurai, and a master of the swift sword. Mr Kawasaki didn't believe in coincidences. Fate had brought them together; he left it to fate to reveal why.

'Hiro, dinner's on the table, don't make me ask twice,' his mother called out from the kitchen. Hiro pulled away from the window and stepped onto the floor. As he did, the floorboards vibrated in time with the penetrating music from below. It was coming from the sake bar. It was always too loud; Hiro banged his foot on the floor in anger and, like always, the sound grew louder.

He banged one more time, just for fun, then went into the kitchen for dinner. There was a single bowl on the table; he was eating alone again. His mother didn't like leaving him, but she was running late for her shift. She worked in a nearby bar operated by the same owner as the bar below; that's how she had managed to rent the box they lived in.

Hiro turned on the small TV on the shelf. The news channel appeared on screen. Before he could change it, his mother stopped him. She was a keen follower of the news, especially beyond Japan – it reminded her of Hiro's father and the places he had seen.

'Turn it up,' she said.

'I thought you were running late?' Hiro replied. She gave him a stare, the one Hiro always obeyed. He turned up the sound, sat back and drank his soup.

The news presenter was reporting a story on an Indian scientist who had published controversial evidence that suggested the Himalayas' northern glaciers were melting at a faster rate than previously recorded. The scientist backed this up with photographic evidence taken over several years showing a large glacier retreating alongside a rising temperature bar. It all sounded very serious.

'Who cares?' muttered Hiro between slurps, each one louder than the last.

'I do,' his mother retorted, 'and so should you: we will all be at the bottom of the sea at this rate.'

The slurping stopped, and she realised her mistake.

'I didn't mean it that way.'

Hiro still had nightmares about his father calling out to him from the sea bed. In the dark water his yellow watch reached out to Hiro before he woke in a sweat.

The new reporter then moved on to the next story.

'In a related story, an archaeological expedition in the northern Himalayas has unearthed historical fragments that are claimed to be several thousand years old. The archaeologist who unearthed the pieces of pottery and miniature carvings believes they belong to an undiscovered ancient civilisation. Professor Anaya Hansen, from the British Museum in London, who made the discovery, told reporters: "We are on the cusp of discovering a lost kingdom, one that is older than any we have found before. The items on display today provide conclusive evidence of an ancient kingdom hidden somewhere in the mountains under thousands of years of snow. As it melts, its secrets are slowly being revealed to the world."'

The news reporter handed back to the presenter, who finished off by saying, 'Professor Hansen's return to the Himalayas followed a four-year absence after her accident during the first expedition. In this expedition, she was caught in an avalanche and badly injured. Afterwards, she was in a coma for some time. It's a remarkable return for Professor Hansen, who until recently had been written off by the archaeological community.'

Hiro's mother was less than impressed. 'The world's melting away and all she cares about is the past! Typical academics, buried in their books and digging for fossils no one cares about. Hiro? Hiro?'

For the first time, he was watching the news. She noticed it too.

'Finish your soup, slowly.'

Hiro swallowed obediently. He had plans for after supper.

'And after you've finished, I want you straight to bed. Apparently you're not getting enough sleep.'

'Who told you that?'

'Your teacher – he said you spend most mornings yawning, half dazed and falling behind in your classwork. It's not good, Hiro; you have to study hard to get a good job one day, like those men in suits outside.'

As much as she wanted him to, Hiro was never going to fall into line and become another suit.

As soon as she left, Hiro finished off the last of his soup in a single gulp. All fuelled up, he went to his room which was lit up by flickering neon lights from the sprawl of electric advertisement boards hanging outside his window. That, along with the pounding beat from the bar below, meant that going to sleep was the last thing on his mind.

Instead Hiro pulled out a games console from under his bed and plugged it in, flexed his fingers, and waited for the game to load on screen. The login page popped up, he entered his screen name and within a second he was in. Leaving behind reality, his mind transcended into the virtual sanctuary of Arya, where he was free to ride on the back of a giant eagle, gliding over the sweeping peaks of the northern mountains and brushing his feet through the turquoise lakes of the lowlands. He was home. Real or not, he believed it was.

Arya was a digital world formulated in the codes of a computer game, an ancient kingdom where millions of teenagers lived out a fantasy existence, as mythical warriors on noble quests. With a single click, Hiro's eagle swept down from the sky and into the heart of a mighty battle. Hiro swung under its beating belly, his right hand gripped his sword, the other held onto the eagle's claw until he was low enough to let go. Before his feet had touched the ground, his sword had claimed three kills with a single strike. Swarmed by legions of the enemy, he raised his sword in defiance and gave a battle cry to alert his friends. Hiro was not alone on this quest, as four others came to his side. Together they charged into battle, to win – or die – for Arya.

The Rishi Scroll – Fall of Arya (Book 1)

therishiscrolls.com - Releasing 2017